PUFFIN BOOKS

Editor: Kaye Webb

BORROBIL

On Beltane Eve Donald and Jean decide to visit the dark mysterious wood on top of the hill. And in the wood they meet Borrobil. As Borrobil explained to them, Beltane is one of the most magic nights of the year, when the White King of Summer must defeat the Black King of Winter. But Borrobil also describes himself as the best *good* magician who ever lived in these parts since the rule of King Diarmid. What better guide could Donald and Jean have to take them to see Morac defeat the poison-breathing Dragon and thence to the north to fetch Princess Finella to be Morac's bride? But the Black Sulig has first to be overcome and when they eventually reach Finella's castle more dangers threaten from the men of the Long Ships.

Donald and Jean return to the wood on the hill just in time to see the fight between the White King and the Black King, and their adventures with Borrobil that Beltane Eve recall the most exciting fairy tales.

For readers between 7 and 10.

Cover illustration by Pauline Baynes

William Croft Dickinson

BORROBIL

ILLUSTRATED BY
JOHN MORTON-SALE

PUFFIN BOOKS
in association with Jonathan Cape

Puffin Books, Penguin Books Ltd, Harmondsworth, Middlesex, England
Penguin Books Inc., 7110 Ambassador Road, Baltimore, Maryland 21207, U.S.A.
Penguin Books Australia Ltd, Ringwood, Victoria, Australia
Penguin Books Canada Ltd, 41 Steelcase Road West, Markham, Ontario, Canada
Penguin Books (N.Z.) Ltd, 182–190 Wairau Road, Auckland 10, New Zealand

—

First published by Jonathan Cape 1944
Published in Puffin Books 1964
Reprinted 1967, 1973, 1976

—

Copyright © William Croft Dickinson, 1944

—

Made and printed in Great Britain
by Richard Clay (The Chaucer Press) Ltd,
Bungay, Suffolk
Set in Monotype Plantin

For
SUSAN and JANE
who were the first
to go through
all these adventures

Contents

CHAPTER I

The Call of the Distant Wood

WHY was the wood so strange and mysterious? There it stood, a dark ring of trees, on the top of the distant hill. It looked much like other woods. Yet there the children had never been. There they so much wanted to go.

Donald and Jean were spending an 'extra' holiday together in an old village where already everyone knew them and they knew everyone. Already, too, they had explored all the meadows, the stream, the water-mill, the duck ponds and the woods; that is, all the woods save one. There it stood, a dark mysterious ring on the crest of the far-off hill.

At first, they had decided to explore it later, when they had finished exploring nearer home. Perhaps it *was* rather far to go. Yet long before they had finished exploring all the exciting places nearer home, they had found that everyone had a different and a special reason why they should keep away from the wood on the distant hill. Even to talk of it seemed certain to bring a warning to stay close by the village and not to venture so far.

Before long, too, they had found that the dark circle of trees had strange and peculiar names. Some called it the 'Eldritch Wood', others called it 'Cauld Coven', while others again called it 'Hathaway Dark'. Even those who just called it 'The Wood' still spoke of it as though it were something more than an ordinary wood, something different from other woods. And it was the one wood where they had never been.

It was all most mysterious. And because it was so mysterious, they began to wonder about the wood. Sometimes it seemed dark and aloof, forbidding, frightening; at other times it appeared lonely and friendless, as though it were longing for someone to visit it and to enter its shade. Soon, as they played in the meadows or round the haystacks, the children found themselves turning to look at it, almost as if it had called to them, whispering to them, 'Come to me. Come to me.' And at night, especially, this call of the wood seemed to be even more urgent, more impelling. Then the children would gaze from their bedroom window at the dark spiky crown breaking the line of the sky until they felt drawn towards it, until they felt they must go and answer its call.

'Oh, I do wish we were going to the wood now, actually now,' said Donald one night as they leaned on their elbows on the window-sill and looked at it longingly from their bedroom window. 'I'm sure it's a magic wood.' Both of them were ready for bed, and they had crept to the window for one last look. The moon was almost at the full, and as he looked, so Donald pictured in his mind exciting adventures on a moonlight night in the midst of the trees. Perhaps there were dwarfs there, cutting down trees for their houses beneath the ground; perhaps he would see fairy smiths at their anvils hammering out magic swords.

'But it may be dangerous,' said Jean cautiously. 'There may be witches there.'

'Nonsense,' answered Donald, speaking with all the authority of an older brother, 'there aren't any witches. Not nowadays anyway. I don't believe anyone can fly through the air just by sitting on an old broom-stick. And even if there were witches there, I'd know what to do if we met them. I'd just cross my fingers and they wouldn't dare to come near us.'

Jean wasn't quite so sure about it. She had a feeling that witches might be more difficult to deal with than that. But she kept silent. Perhaps Donald was right after all. She looked again at the wood, and now the tall trees standing stark and straight against the lighter sky seemed to be holding out long arms to bid them 'Come; come to us.'

Suddenly she felt afraid, but at that moment Donald jumped up and cried out eagerly, 'Jean, let's go; let's go to-night! No one would hear us if we crept out by the back staircase. It would be easy to find our way in the moonlight. Do say you'll come.'

Jean stood up more slowly, and looked at Donald wonder-ingly. To go to the wood alone? And at night? What if those tall black trees were to hold them and keep them? Perhaps there weren't any witches, but there might yet be something else hidden away in that strange darkness.

'Will it be safe?' she said at length.

'Of course,' answered Donald. 'And I'll look after you.' Again Jean wasn't so sure about it; then, all at once, her doubts and her fears seemed to vanish and she felt quite brave.

'Well, I could take my lucky-stone,' she said, 'and then we'd be all right.'

'Yes,' cried Donald. 'Bring your lucky-stone with you. We'll go tonight. We may not get another chance.'

Jean gave one more look at the black ring of trees on the far-off hill. But now she had made up her mind. She began to dress, though perhaps more slowly, more deliberately than Donald. Soon the two of them were creeping quietly down the staircase that led straight to the backdoor of the house. In her right hand Jean clutched tightly her 'lucky-stone' – a brownish-yellowish 'pebble' that looked like a stone and yet was not a stone. What it was the children had no idea. But Jean had picked it up in one of the fields some days before and she had carried it about with her as her 'lucky-stone' ever since. Donald, more practical, and also always more hungry, had put three biscuits in his pocket – nice large biscuits with a picture of a wheatsheaf on them – all that remained of the 'food reserve' he had built up from the biscuit-barrel on the dining-room sideboard.

No creaking came from the stairs to betray them. As they passed by the kitchen they could hear the grown-ups talking there. Donald paused for a moment, but the only word he could catch sounded like 'Beltane'. Jean was already outside the door and in the night. Donald joined her, and pulled-to the door. 'Beltane,' he thought, 'what a funny word. I wonder if it's another of those queer names for the wood?'

CHAPTER 2

The Way to the Wood and What They Found There

THEIR way lay across the meadows at the back of the house. That part was easy. The path showed up clearly in the moonlight, and they could even see the dark shapes of the cows as they lay in the longer grass by the dyke. Over the first stile, across the second meadow, and down to the haystacks. They had been there before. It would have been nice to stay and play round the haystacks in the moonlight; but their journey was to the wood. So on they went. Over the stile and across the third meadow. Then another stile. And now they had never been so far before.

They climbed the third stile and found themselves in a narrow lane that led up the hill towards the wood. Now was the real beginning of their adventure. The lane twisted and turned, this way and that. Soon it was so narrow that Donald had to walk ahead with Jean following. On either side of them the hedgerows became thicker and thicker; and as they thickened so they began to bend over the lane, meeting one another overhead and forming a dark ceiling above two dark walls. Scarcely any moonlight came through. The lane was steep, narrow and dark. Before long, Jean noticed that it was silent, too. In the undergrowth on either side there were no rustling and squeaking noises such as she had always heard in the evening hedgerows. All was quiet and still. Even their own footsteps made no sound. They seemed to be walking in soft shoes along a dark passage that had no ending; and no beginning either, for as they looked behind them they could see nothing but a wall of blackness that cut them off from the way they had come. Both were a little frightened. It would have been easier, perhaps, if they could have walked together; but the lane grew narrower and narrower. Jean clutched her lucky-stone tightly in her right hand, and began to wish she was at home again and in her warm bed. Once or twice with her other hand she had been able to hold on to Donald's coat; but the lane seemed determined to keep them apart, and as often as she gained a hold she found herself forced to let go. Even Donald, trying hard to feel brave, still could not help feeling as though he was pushing his way against a soft blackness that retreated before him only to creep round behind him; a blackness that surrounded them and shut them in; a blackness mysteriously determined to prevent them from reaching the wood.

Now, too, they noticed that the hill was much steeper than it had looked. From time to time they were scrambling on hands and knees, and at one point they were climbing what seemed to be the rough face of a dry-stone wall. Jean, though tough and sturdy, was quite worn out. Her lip was quivering, and the tears were ready to come.

'Oh, Donald,' she cried at last, 'I can't climb any more. I'm all betired.'

'We'll get to the end of this one bit,' said Donald, setting his teeth, 'and then we'll sit down for a rest. We may have to give it up, but I'd rather not, when we have come so far. Come on, Jean, one bit more.' Yet even Donald felt that he could scarcely go one step farther; the journey to the wood was proving far different from all that he had imagined it would be.

And then, strangely enough, the lane which seemed as though it were determined to obstruct them when they wanted to push on, now seemed just as determined to help them when they were on the point of giving in and turning back. For even as he spoke, Donald sensed that in that 'one bit more' the lane widened, and at the same time he knew that they had reached level ground. Jean caught up with him and he took her hand. Now the hedgerows seemed thinner and higher; weak shafts of moonlight came through; they could see that the low trees and shrubs of the lane were giving way to tall firs standing wide apart. They were in the wood! But it was still almost as dark as it had been in the lane, and underneath their feet a thick carpet of pine-needles deadened all sound.

'What do we do now?' asked Jean in a whisper.

'I don't know,' answered Donald, though he was half inclined to say that perhaps now they could turn round and go back home again. After all, they *had* been to the wood, they had even been inside it. They had done all they had set out to do.

For a short while they stood irresolute, peering into the semi-darkness. But the blackness of the wood was still almost as impenetrable as the blackness of the lane, and all they could see were the trunks of the nearest fir trees standing bare beside them. Everything was dark and quiet and still. Then, faintly, a long way off, there came a single call. Donald heard it and looked at Jean. He saw that Jean also had heard something. They drew closer together, feeling for each other's hands. Both of them listened. It came again. This time there could be no mistake. Someone, something, had called somewhere in the depths of the wood. For what seemed to them a long time they stood together, peering and listening. But all was silence. Not even a breath of wind stirred the branches of the trees. Then, as they strove to pierce the darkness ahead, as they stood anxious and not a little afraid, two small red lights suddenly appeared in the far distance. The lights flickered; now they seemed to be moving up and down. Jean's heart began to thump. Witches? Wolves? But the two lights quickly grew brighter and larger, and all at once Donald, relieved, cried 'Fires!' Two big fires were burning amid the trees ahead.

What should they do now? Should they walk towards those fires, or should they turn round and try to make their way home? Jean looked at the two fires ahead and Jean made up her mind. 'It was such a long climb,' she said, 'and I've got my lucky-stone.' Donald knew her well enough to know that that meant she was not going home until they had done something to make up for that long and wearying climb. And doing something meant going forward to explore the fires. If Jean could go, well, he could go, too.

They began to walk on again. As they went their journey

became easier and easier. Once more it seemed as if the wood,
like the lane, was determined to make up for the labour that
had gone before. No fallen trees barred the way. The firs
seemed to stand wider and wider apart, so that now the clear

moonlight came through. Soon there was the added light from
the fires ahead. When first they had seen the fires they had
seemed to be a long way off; now their walk to them seemed to
be over almost as soon as it had begun.

They found themselves standing on the edge of a round
clearing in the wood. In the centre of the clearing stood a low

circular mound surrounded by a shallow trench. On the mound itself stood a ring of nine tall stones. And the two fires of blazing pine-logs, burned brightly before what looked like the entrance to the ring. There was no one to be seen.

'Oh! But it's lovely,' cried Jean.

Donald, feeling the responsibility of older years, stood looking and wondering. What could it mean? Who had lit the fires? Why the mound and trench? Why that circle of nine tall stones? But Jean was not to be held back. There, in between the fires, in front of the entrance to the ring of stones, she could see a rough flight of steps cut into the bank of the mound. She ran forward even as Donald called to her to come back. In between the fires, up the steps in the bank of the mound, straight between the two tallest stones of the ring she ran. And then, in and out of the standing stones she danced, wildly, backwards and forwards, the fires throwing strange shadows on the white stones as she passed them to and fro.

Donald walked forward slowly, frowning and wondering.

'Jean,' he called. 'Perhaps we shouldn't have come here.'

'But Donald, feel how lovely the grass is; and see how white the big stones look in the light of the fires.'

Again she danced round and round and in and out the stones of the ring. Tiring at last, she came back to Donald who had now climbed the mound to reach her, but who was still looking puzzled and doubtful, still half-wishing they had not entered the ring.

'And we're here, all by ourselves, in the wood at last,' panted Jean.

'Good morning,' said a strange voice. And at the self-same moment the fires of burning pine-logs disappeared; the standing-stones seemed to become higher and more majestic; the ring itself seemed to become wider and more spacious; the night seemed to change to the half-light of dawn; and a fresh wind blew.

CHAPTER 3

Enter Borrobil

'GOOD morning, for the second time,' said the voice, adding half musingly, half playfully –

> *'If at first there's no reply*
> *Try again; they may be shy.'*

Donald and Jean had both jumped when the strange voice had said 'Good morning,' and when everything around them

had suddenly changed. But with this second greeting, some-how or other they felt that whoever he was he was friendly, and probably nice. Their first fright began to disappear. Both of them looked round, to right, to left, behind them; but there was no one to be seen. All around them were the trees of the wood, and even though the wood did seem different from what it had been, it was still the wood at any rate.

'Good morning, for the third time,' said the voice.

'But where are you?' cried Donald.

'Here I am,' said the voice.

Both the children looked eagerly about, but still there was no one to be seen.

'Oh dear,' sighed Jean, 'I do wish we could see you.'

'And so you shall,' said the voice. And stepping from behind a tree almost in front of them, came the merriest, queerest little man Donald and Jean had ever seen. His eyes were bright and sparkling; his mouth looked as though it was just about to break open in a large and mischievous grin; and although in one way he looked as though he must have lived for hundreds of years, in another way he looked as young as they themselves. He was dressed entirely in brown, and as soon as he stepped out he gave both of them a deep bow, sweeping the ground in front of him with his pointed hat in the tip of which a white owl's feather bobbed to and fro.

'Good morning. Borrobil is the name. And at your service.'

'Good morning. I'm Donald.'

'And I'm Jean.'

'And now we all know one another,' said Borrobil; and again he bowed, sweeping the ground with his hat.

For a moment there was silence as the children looked at Borrobil and Borrobil looked at the children.

'I think I like you,' confided Jean at last. 'But why did you say "Good morning" when it must be quite late at night?'

'Yes,' added Donald, knowing that to talk about the weather was much the best way of beginning any conversation 'And why has the night suddenly changed and become like morning? It seems funny, somehow.'

'But surely,' replied Borrobil, 'surely you knew what would happen when you ran between the Beltane Fires and danced in the Nine-Stone-Ring?'

'No,' answered Donald. 'We weren't expecting anything to happen at all. Isn't "Beltane" just another name for the wood, for this wood, I mean? Is it something quite different?'

Borrobil seemed puzzled. He looked from Donald to Jean, and back from Jean to Donald. He looked at both of them together. Then slowly he put on his hat.

'Beltane,' he said, and by the way he spoke it sounded dreadfully important. 'Beltane means the end of the Black King's rule and the beginning of the White King's reign.'

It was now the turn of Donald and Jean to feel puzzled. Neither of them knew what to say. They looked at Borrobil much as though he had asked them a riddle to which they felt there could be no answer.

'I don't know what you mean,' confessed Donald at last.

'But,' said Borrobil, 'it's very important to know these things. If you don't know them you'll never know where you are.'

Donald and Jean felt they didn't know where they were anyway; but they were hardly prepared for what happened next. Borrobil gave them one more look and then suddenly began:

> '*Dig the ditch and raise the mound;*
> *Form the ring in elfin ground.*
> *Light the fires of burning brands*
> *Where the Nine-Stone-Circle stands.*

> '*Who dare pass the fires between?*
> *Who dare reach the magic green?*
> *Who dare dance on magic ground*
> *In the Nine-Stone-Circle round?*

> '*On Beltane Eve when eagles fly*
> *On awful errands through the sky,*
> *The White King's host will win the fight*
> *And put the Black King's horde to flight.*

> '*Black is death, cold Winter's black;*
> *White is life, warm Summer's white.*
> *The Beltane trees with burning light*
> *Bid Winter flee, call Summer back.*

'Who will pass the fires between?
Who will dance on magic green?
He shall see the long ago
Beyond the Circle's Beltane glow.'

'So there you are; or perhaps I should say "Here you are." And here's Borrobil to be your guide; and, if I may modestly say so, your guide is the best *good* magician who has lived in these parts ever since the rule of King Diarmid.' And Borrobil made another deep bow, again sweeping the ground with his hat, in the tip of which the white owl's feather seemed to bob up and down, as though nodding its head to say 'Yes; yes; that's right; that's right'.

'But whatever does it all mean?' asked Donald.

And as for Jean, she looked at Borrobil with sparkling eyes and chimed in, 'Oh, I do wish you'd say another one.'

Borrobil looked crestfallen. 'Oh dear,' he said, 'didn't you follow it all? And I made that song myself. I thought it was quite clear as well as being quite a good song. But perhaps I'd better explain it all another way. Don't you know that Beltane Eve is the last night of Winter, the last night before Summer reigns again? Don't you know that *every* year on Beltane Eve the White King of Summer *must* defeat the Black King of Winter, however strong the Black King may be? Every year the White King sends out his Heralds of Spring to announce his coming. Then the grass begins to grow and the trees begin to bud; the lambs frisk; and the young birds begin to cheep. But the Black King is not easy to overthrow; not easily does he give up his reign. Sometimes he fights back with storms and floods; sometimes with bitter frosts and biting winds he drives back the Heralds of Spring. Then for a while he laughs, and rules again. Then the grass blackens once more, the buds wither and shrink, the young ones die. But always the White King of Summer is marching on; and every year on Beltane Eve he meets the Black King of Winter, defeats him in the fight, and drives him out of the land, making him flee to the other side of the world. So it goes on, year by year. And so the flowers that have been dead all winter come to life again each

year when the King of Summer has won. For the Black King
of Winter rules with cold and death, but the White King of
Summer brings warmth and life. And on this important night,
on Beltane Eve, you've passed between the watch-fires of the
White King's camp, and you've danced inside his Nine-Stone-
Ring where he will fight against the Black King and where he
will drive him out of the land. And to do that, to enter the
White King's camp and to dance *with summer joy* on the very
night on which the Black King will at last be overthrown, is
about the most magic-making thing I know. It's like telling the
White King that he's won already, or the Black King that he
simply cannot win. In fact it's so magic-making that you have
now come back to see for a while the times that are dead, and
then, when the Black King who rules in death has been defeated and driven out, you will go back again to the White
King's summer and to the times that live.'

'It all sounds very befusing,' muttered Jean.

But Donald thought he understood. 'Do you mean,' he
asked, 'that we are now in the times that are dead and gone,
and that we shall see lots of things that happened long ago?'

'Right!' answered Borrobil. 'And when the White King has
fought the Black King and has made him flee the land, then
you will go back again from death to life, from the past to the
present. You will find yourselves back again by the Beltane
Fires in the Wood. That's why the darkness of your night
suddenly changed to the light of a past day. That's why I said
"Good morning" when you thought I ought to have said
"Good evening". And now I come to think of it, a "Good
morning" it is too. It looks like being a fine day. And Morac
looks like having the sun with him when he fights the dragon.'

'Dragon!' cried Donald and Jean together. 'Where? When?'

'Morac fights the long dragon today,' answered Borrobil.
'If you will come with me . . .'

But he was interrupted by such a hurrying and a scurrying,
such a rushing and a crushing, with shouts and the blowing of
horns and bugles, and the galloping of horses that his last words
were completely drowned. Donald and Jean ran to the nearest

tree, and stood behind it, looking in all directions and wondering how they could avoid such a mad tumult of galloping horses. But although the horsemen seemed to be all around them and even on top of them, there was nothing to be seen. And almost as quickly as the troop had come upon them the last horseman had ridden by and all was quiet again. Borrobil came running up, looking most contrite and yet unable to conceal a mischievous gleam in his eyes.

'It's all right,' he said, 'that was only King Eochaid riding by with his men. Often does he pass this way on his never-ending ride through all the land, so that now we are well accustomed to his troop. But never before have I known him ride in the early light of dawn: though that may well be due to the day itself – the last day of the seventh year; the day when the dragon waits.'

'But they did sound close,' cried Donald.

'Yes,' answered Borrobil. 'And yet though they ride the earth, no man has seen the hoof-mark of their horses, no man has seen broken grass or bended heather in their wake.'

Donald was just going to say 'Why?' when Jean interrupted, 'But are they always riding? Won't they get tired?'

'Yes, they are always riding and yet they never tire,' answered Borrobil, seriously. 'And I'm afraid they must go on riding for long years to come. For the White Dog has not jumped down.'

'Whatever are you talking about?' asked Donald, rather crossly, for he still felt a little ashamed of having taken shelter behind a tree, and he thought that Borrobil was purposely trying to confuse them. 'What dog? And why should it jump down? And why is the last day of the seventh year different from all other days?'

Borrobil looked at him as though he scarcely knew what answer to make.

'And why does King Somebody-or-other keep on riding with a White Dog?' persisted Jean.

'Stop, stop!' cried Borrobil. 'Here are too many questions for one answer.' Then, more reflectively, 'But I suppose that

now you are here you really ought to know about all these
things. And I suppose there's just about time to tell you. But
you will have to put your best foot forward as soon as I've
finished. For I have yet to find a man called Giric whom I
must take to Morac before he fights the dragon. And of Giric's
counsel Morac stands in great need. That, indeed, is the most
important thing of all. Still, if you do want to hear about King
Eochaid, even before we've found Giric and set out for the
Dragon's Hollow . . .'

This seemed to set them a difficult choice.

'I'd sooner see the dragon-fight,' said Donald, and he looked
at Jean, for he knew that Jean was always ready to listen to a
story of any kind.

'But we can still hear the story of the King and the White
Dog, and still be in time for the dragon-fight, can't we?' she
asked. Borrobil nodded his head.

'Oh, please then,' cried Jean.

'Well, as long as we don't miss the dragon . . .,' continued
Donald.

Borrobil looked up at the sky, just as he might have looked
at a watch. 'No, we shan't do that,' he answered. And then
motioning the children to sit down at the foot of a tall fir he
sat down beside them and began the old old story of King
Eochaid and the White Dog.

CHAPTER 4

The Story of King Eochaid

'THIS then is the story of King Eochaid,' began Borrobil:

Hundreds of years ago (and that's long before I was a magician's apprentice and just beginning to learn my trade) King Eochaid ruled over these and all the neighbouring lands as far as his sword could reach. Now it happened one day, as King Eochaid was riding past a small grassy knoll, that suddenly he saw a stranger, riding towards him on a brown goat. As the stranger drew nearer the king could see that he was small of stature, with a long red beard, and ears the size of a man's hand. And when they met they greeted one another courteously.

'Well met, King Eochaid,' said the stranger. 'Although I am unknown to you, yet am I a king in my own land, and I should take it as an honour to be invited to your wedding-feast.'

'But it is news to me that I am to wed at all,' replied King Eochaid. 'And surely I must find my bride before inviting guests to my wedding-feast. But since you say it would be an honour to be invited, then gladly do I invite you. Though when my wedding-feast will take place is another matter altogether.'

'Thank you,' said the stranger, gravely, 'and I should count it as an honour if you would attend my own wedding-feast, one year after your own.'

All this seemed naught but madness to King Eochaid, but equally gravely he replied that that was a bargain and a bargain that he would keep. And no sooner had he so replied than the stranger on the brown goat completely vanished.

At this the king was much troubled, for he knew now that he had met the Fairy King, and still anxious in his mind, he turned his horse round to make his way home. But scarcely had he reached the sea-coast near which his castle stood, than he saw something out to sea which looked like a boat and yet was not a boat. Then he saw that it was gradually drawing nearer to the land. He had keen eyes, and as he looked he was amazed to see that it was a woman riding upon the back of a grey seal. She appeared to be of great beauty and she seemed to ride her strange craft lightly and easily. Reaching the shallow waters of the shore, she alighted, with the water to her knees; and the grey seal plunged and disappeared. And now King Eochaid could see that she was the loveliest woman his eyes had ever gazed upon. For a long time he stood silent, speechless before the sight of that lovely face. Then he said, 'Welcome to my land, fair lady. But tell me why you come in this strange way, riding the waters of the sea upon the back of a seal?'

'I am called Irmin,' the lady replied. 'And my father is king over all Domnania. With many knights from my father's court, I was sailing on a visit to my uncles in Ardgal when our ship was overtaken by a violent storm. For long the sailors drove her before the wind, but at last, one wave, greater than all that had gone before, seemed to rise up behind us and towering high above our mast fell upon the ship with such force that she was broken into two and so sank. Then was I like to have perished with the rest had I not known a magic spell which brought the King of the Seals to my aid.'

Then to this fair maiden King Eochaid was drawn by all the cords of love. And she, loving him in turn, their wedding feast was proclaimed to all, and all made welcome to attend.

But when Eochaid and Irmin took their seats at the head of the feast, and all was ready to begin, then, even before the first dish had been placed upon the tables, the dwarf king of the red beard suddenly presented himself, and with him so many other dwarfs in his following that seats could not be found for one tenth of them. Yet this the dwarfs themselves quickly remedied, for in a moment they had raised large pavilions of the finest silk and in them seats and tables sufficient for all and as many more as cared to come. In and out of the pavilions rushed the servants of the dwarf king, bearing vessels and goblets, each fashioned out of a single precious stone, so that all ate and drank from diamonds, emeralds and rubies, and from sapphires, amethysts and pearls; and none handled wood or horn. Of food, too, nought was lacking, but every dish was of the rarest savour, sweet and of delicious taste. And, indeed, the servants of King Eochaid were never called upon to bring out the many dishes that had been stored high in the royal larder. All was provided by the dwarfs; all were served by the

servants of the dwarfs; all ate and drank from the dwarfs' vessels. And everyone wondered; not the least of their wonders being the precious stones in their hands, and over all the clothing and bright jewels of the dwarf king and his following that made them shine like so many brilliant lamps at the feast.

At last the feast drew towards its close, and the dwarf king rose to depart. Then turning to King Eochaid he said: 'All men are witness, King Eochaid, that you have honoured me by welcoming me at your wedding-feast; and to you, I and my court have done all honour that we could. Let all men know that one year hence I shall honour you at my own wedding-feast, there to return to me what honour you can.' And with these words he and his following left the feast-tables, and no man saw which way they went.

One year went by; and on the last day of the year two dwarfs appeared as messengers before King Eochaid inviting him to the wedding-feast of their own king. Eochaid, mindful of his bargain, accepted their invitation; and though his heart was troubled within him, yet he gathered together the great men of his court, with rich presents and an abundance of food and wine. And with his following he rode with the dwarf King's messengers.

Their way took them to a high rock, and through a door marvellously cut therein, which brought them into a passage of black darkness down which they rode singly until at length it opened out into a multitude of pleasant halls lit by a thousand and one lamps of different colours. Here they dismounted from their horses. Here the dwarf king himself welcomed them, and with great courtesy led them to the feast. And at the feast King Eochaid and his men played no small part. Yet however much they ate, the food never seemed to grow less; no matter how often they poured out the wine, the flagons were never empty.

At last the feast drew towards its close, and King Eochaid and his following rose to depart. The dwarf King himself accompanied them as far as the passage of black darkness. Here their horses were brought to them; and here the dwarf king presented to Eochaid a white dog to carry, strictly warning him that on no account must any of his men dismount from their horses until the white dog had jumped from his arms. And with that the dwarf king took leave of Eochaid.

Within a short space King Eochaid and his men reached once more the light of the sun; and seeing an old shepherd the king accosted him, asking him for news of Irmin his queen. Then did the shepherd turn to Eochaid with astonishment; he looked at him for long without speaking; at last he said: 'Sir,

I can hardly follow your speech, for it is strange to me; and of Queen Irmin I know little, save that once I heard how long ago there was a queen of that name who was married to King Eochaid; and he, men say, disappeared with all his knights into the face of this very rock, led there by a pigmy. But that must have been full one hundred years before this day, and Queen Irmin must have been gathered to her grave wellnigh as many years ago.'

The king, who thought he had made a stay of but one night, could scarcely believe his ears. Some of his company, astounded at what the shepherd said, leapt from their horses to the ground. But the white dog had not jumped from the king's arms, and all those who touched the earth were in a moment turned to dust. Eochaid, seeing this, and understanding all that happened to him and to his men, warned the rest of them to ride on with him and not to alight from their horses until the white dog in his arms had first jumped down.

But Eochaid still rides with his men throughout the land, for the white dog has not yet left his arms.

Borrobil paused. Then, in a different tone and as if talking to himself: 'And it was Eochaid, still riding, who passed us with his troop. Yet never before have I known him ride in the grey light of dawn. And this is the last day of the seventh year. Is the portent good or ill? Who knows? Yet something tells me that today all will be well, and well with Morac.'

Suddenly he jumped to his feet, startling the children whose minds were still full of all that he had said and told. 'We must be off,' he cried. 'We must find Giric and with him we must reach Morac before he sets out to fight the dragon. Do you still want to come?'

'Yes! Yes!' they cried at once.

'Up then,' he said. And as they stood up Donald felt certain he heard Borrobil say something beneath his breath that seemed to end with the words,

> '*May Morac win*
> *The Dragon-skin.*'

CHAPTER 5

The Dragon; and How it Came

'WHICH way do we go?' asked Donald.

'Trust me,' answered Borrobil. 'I know every path of the wood. I know the rabbit's path, the hare's path, the fox's path, and the wolf's path. I know the bear's path, the path of deer and the path of men. I know the eagle's way and the way of the dragons that fly. And the first way for us is the way to Giric's house.' And saying this he set off through the tall firs, with the two children following.

Now it was broad daylight; and again the wood looked much like all other woods. Perhaps there were more tangles of low undergrowth; but Borrobil clearly knew the path, for always, even in what looked like the very thickest mass of tangled growth, he seemed to make unerringly for the one way through. Before long they struck a rough track which wound in and out of the trees and skirted the tangled masses of undergrowth. Now it was possible for Donald and Jean to walk abreast of their guide, and now Donald seized the opportunity for which he had been waiting.

'Is Giric's house a big house?' he asked. 'Will it have a moat all round it, and towers and battlements like a castle?'

'No,' answered Borrobil shortly. 'It is an earth-house. You will see it when we get there.'

Obviously, as he had warned them, he was anxious that they should 'put their best foot forward'. But Jean, too, had been waiting to put a question.

'Please,' she said, 'will it be a *geesty* dragon?'

Borrobil stopped short, and looked at her. But Donald laughed. 'That's only one of Jean's words,' he explained. 'It means something that's horrible and nasty and terrible and fierce.'

'Yes,' said Borrobil, walking slowly on again. 'Long and nasty and horrible and fierce. That's why Morac fights it today; that's why countless other brave men have fought it in the past, though alas, so far always in vain. Already it has devoured its thousands and tens of thousands of cattle and sheep and men, so that even long years ago the people of the kingdom were reduced to a small number and the rest fled in terror before it, leaving it to rule the kingdom by itself, but a kingdom almost barren of man and beast.'

For a while the children were silent. Then Jean, looking straight ahead of her, asked again, and in a small voice, 'Will it have *climpers*, Borrobil?'

He turned to her with a puzzled look, and Donald once more explained. 'That's only another of Jean's words. You'll soon get used to them. *Climpers* means something that clutches and pinches at one and the same time.'

'Even its breath does that,' answered Borrobil gravely. 'Those who come within reach of its breath are lost, for they are drawn down its throat. Its breath reaches out and seizes them even as a frog will catch flies with its tongue.'

They walked on in silence.

'Morac *is* a strong man, isn't he?' asked Jean.

'Yes, very strong.'

A further silence. Then Jean again:

'But *we* shall be safe, shan't we?'

Borrobil smiled at her comfortingly. 'I shall look after you,' he said; 'and did I not say I was the best *good* magician who has lived in these parts ever since the rule of King Diarmid?' And with that he quickened his pace again, so much so that first Jean and then Donald soon fell behind. Also they were much taken up with their own thoughts, and particularly with thoughts of the dragon. From time to time they looked at Borrobil striding ahead. And then, suddenly, he had disappeared. He was nowhere to be seen! They both stopped. He had vanished, just as if the earth had opened up and swallowed him.

'Borrobil, Borrobil,' they called.

There was no answer. Jean put her hand to her mouth.

'It's all right,' said Donald reassuringly; 'he can't be far away. I think he was just by that low mound when we last saw him. At any rate we can walk there first, and if we climb it perhaps we shall be able to see him.'

They ran to the mound, and Donald was just reaching up to climb with hands and feet, when out popped Borrobil right in front of him. He jumped back with a start. But before he had time to become even the least bit cross, the little man grinned one of his largest grins, and telling Jean to hold on to Donald's hand he took Donald's other hand in his own and so led them behind the mound and through a narrow opening of two upright stones in the side of the grassy slope. They turned, first left, then right, and immediately they were in pitch darkness. At once Donald guessed that this must be the entrance to Giric's 'earth-house'; and almost as if to support his guess, Borrobil called out:

'Giric! There are friends in your house. Borrobil is here.'

In answer to the call, the children saw a faint light in the distance which soon became a funny oil-lamp, rather like a small saucer with a bit of cloth burning in it. Then they saw that the lamp was carried by a man, thick-set and strong, who seemed to be coming out of a long low passage in which he had to bend down as he walked, and which was completely lined with big slabs of stone. Overhead Donald noticed that the roof had been made by balancing stones one upon the other until they met in the middle, so that it looked as though the man was walking to them down an old-fashioned beehive built of stones. 'A beehive for moles,' he thought to himself, and grinned. But as the light from the lamp came closer he could see that all of them were standing in the same stone passage themselves.

'Greetings, Borrobil,' said the man.

'And to thee, Giric,' answered Borrobil. 'Greetings to thee also from Donald and Jean'; and he pointed to the children standing beside him.

Donald held out his hand, and was just going to say, 'How do you do?' when Jean broke in:

'What a funny tunnel! Wherever does it go?'

'Tunnel?' said Giric.

'Yes, where we are now,' said Jean.

Giric looked at her. 'It doesn't go anywhere,' he said.

'But it must,' persisted Jean, 'I saw you coming out of it.'

Borrobil laughed. 'It's all right, Giric,' he said, 'they are strangers to the land; all things are new to them.' Then, turning to Jean, he continued, 'This isn't a tunnel, although it may look like one. This is Giric's house; it's his earth-house. Though, of course, he'll be leaving it any time now.'

'Why; has someone else taken it?' asked Jean.

Again Borrobil laughed. 'No, no,' he said. 'This is Giric's *winter* house. You see Giric still believes in the old customs and the old ways. And because he keeps to the old customs and the old ways of living, every winter he retires to his earth-house, which probably looks to you like a long stone-lined tunnel, and nothing more. But it's really quite warm in winter, and it's safe from the wolves and other dangers of the black days. Moreover, Giric not only keeps to the old customs and the old ways, but also he knows far more about olden things than anyone else. And that means that he knows far more about the ways of the dragon than anyone else. All of which is the reason why Morac asked me to find him and to bring him with me so that Morac could take counsel with him before the fight.'

All this time Giric had been standing by, looking as though everything that Borrobil had to say was of no interest to him at all. But as soon as Borrobil mentioned the dragon and the fight his aloofness vanished. His eyes lit up. Here was something worth listening to! Borrobil, like the children, noticed the change; and turning to him, Borrobil said, 'This is the last day of the seventh year. And Morac waits.'

'Good,' cried Giric. 'Has Morac made ready?'

'Yes. All is ready.'

'Then let us go, for we waste time in waiting.' And Giric hastily passed through the narrow opening of his house, Borrobil and the children following him.

Like Borrobil he seemed to know the way, for he pushed

quickly ahead; though Jean was glad that it was Giric, and not Borrobil, who was now leading them. She found it much easier to keep pace with Giric. Moreover, the trees were now thinning and there were more open spaces, so they could all walk together in a small group instead of one behind the other. And here it should be added that walking one behind another in single file was something Jean simply hated, for it nearly always meant that she came last, and then if she wanted to stop and look at something the others would be urging her to come on; whereas if those in front wanted to stop and look at something, she had to stop too, whether she wanted to look or not.

'How will Morac kill the dragon?' she asked, turning to Borrobil.

'I don't know,' he answered. 'And we don't even know that he *will* kill it. Many brave men have tried to kill it in the past, but so far all have failed. And all the dragons I have seen killed have all been killed in different ways, for every dragon is different from every other dragon, and no two dragons fight alike. But Giric is wiser in these things than I am. Perhaps Giric can tell us?'

But Giric walked on without a word. 'Taciturn,' said Donald to himself, 'I'm sure that's the right word.'

Jean, however, was not to be silenced by Giric's unwillingness to talk.

'But how was the last dragon killed?' she asked. 'I mean the last dragon *you* saw being killed.'

Borrobil looked at her. 'What a lot of questions you ask, and what a lot of answers you expect,' he said. 'And just when we should be saving our breath to get on as fast as we can. Let me see now. Yes, I remember the last one. But it wasn't exactly killed; it killed itself.'

'Killed itself!' echoed Donald and Jean.

'Yes, like the dragon Morac will fight today, that dragon was always hungry; and that proved its undoing. It lived in a large cave by the sea-shore, and every few days out it would come from its cave, seize as many cattle and men as it could, take them back to its cave, and so fill up its larder from the top shelf right down to the bottom one. But always before many days had gone by the larder would be empty again, for it was very greedy, as well as being always hungry, and then out it would come from its cave again, to seize anything it could. And this went on and on, but nobody knew how to persuade the dragon to move to some other district, or failing that, how to kill it. Moreover, it was impossible to kill it when it was asleep after one of its heavy meals (as many a dragon has been killed in the past), for this dragon never went to sleep until it had drawn itself into a narrow opening at the back of the cave, an opening too narrow for any man to get through, unless he crawled in flat along the floor; and no man was found brave enough to do that. But, in the end, Coll the fisherman brought it to destruction.

'About the time when he judged its larder would be nearly empty, Coll anchored his boat opposite the entrance to the dragon's cave. Then, by fastening barrels together with ropes, he made a bridge of barrels from his boat to the shore. But into each barrel of his bridge he drove cruel spikes, so that, when he began to roast an ox on his boat, and when the fragrant smell of roasting ox began to reach the dragon, and when the dragon began to cross the bridge (for it was always hungry), then did the spikes in the barrels tear deep into its body as it persisted in trying to reach the boat (for it was always greedy). But still it went on, tearing deep gashes in its body, and almost had it reached the last barrel of Coll's bridge when Coll, weighing anchor, sailed away from his bridge, so that now there was a wide gap between the bridge of barrels and the boat, a gap too wide for the dragon to leap.

'The savoury smell of roasting ox still came from the boat to the nostrils of the dragon; but already it had torn its body almost to pieces to get to that roasting ox, and now it could neither leap across the waters to the boat nor return across the spikes to the shore. If it leapt it would drown; if it returned across the spikes it would certainly tear itself to death. On the last barrel of Coll's bridge the dragon looked to seaward and to landward; but neither way could it go. On the last barrel of Coll's bridge the dragon died of starvation and loss of blood.'

Donald eyed Borrobil rather curiously. At one moment it looked as though he was going to say, 'I don't believe a single word of it,' but apparently he changed his mind. Instead, he asked, 'Well, where do dragons come from, anyway?'

'From different places and in different ways,' answered Borrobil. 'They are all different. No two dragons come in the same way and no dragon . . .'

'Well, where did this one come from that Morac will fight today?' interrupted Donald, for Borrobil's beginning sounded much too familiar.

Borrobil sighed. 'You are as bad as Jean,' he said. 'The

dragon that Morac fights today came from a tiny egg brought
by a black eagle in its beak. That was a long long time ago.
The eagle circled round and round in the sky, and at length
alighted on the tower of King Diarmid's castle. From there it
dropped to the castle-gate where Diarmid was holding his
court. And while all men watched it in wonder, it placed the
egg at the king's feet and then, with a cry, soared away and
disappeared. And thereupon much talking was there in Diarmid's court. Some of the wise men were of opinion that the
black eagle was a bird of ill-omen, and that the egg which it
had carried in its beak should be crushed forthwith. And those
wise men said the egg would bring no good but great evil.
Others of the wise men, however, were of opinion that the eagle
had brought the egg to King Diarmid as the greatest king in
the land, and that it had placed the egg in his safe-keeping and
that one day it would return for it. And those wise men said
that the egg would bring no evil, but great good. And so was
there much arguing. But Diarmid, great king as he was, was
only a man after all. And it flattered him to think that the egg
had been brought to him as the greatest of all kings, for him
to guard it with all his might. Thus the egg was not crushed,
but it was placed on a velvet cushion in the king's chamber.
There it lay for seven full years. And at the end of the seventh
year the egg cracked, and out of it came a small golden worm.

'Again there was argument, and much talk in King Diarmid's
court; but again the end of it was that the worm was not
crushed, but it was placed in a golden casket in the king's
treasury. There it grew in size until the casket was no longer
large enough to hold it. A silver cradle was then its home; but
as it grew, the cradle in turn became too small for it, and it was
placed in a crystal chest. In turn the crystal chest became too
small, and the worm occupied one of the long halls of the castle
where it still continued to grow.

'And now all men knew that an evil thing had come among
them and had been cherished by them. And all men, including
King Diarmid himself, were sore afraid of the worm that had
broken out of the egg brought by the black eagle, and that now

had grown until it filled one of the castle halls. A council was held, and it was agreed to kill the worm lest, as it grew, it should take over the whole of the king's castle. Then was there drawing of lots to decide who should kill the worm: and the

lot fell on Diarmid himself. Boldly the king went to the long hall where the worm lay. But it turned upon him; its breath melted his sword and shield; and only the magic armour he wore saved the king from being himself shrivelled up like a leaf that is caught in the fire.

'Consternation now ruled in Diarmid's court. Another

council was held. Then as all men talked, an old man approached the place of the Council and begged to be heard. He was
given permission to speak, and speaking, said that even as the
egg of the worm had been brought in the first place by the
black eagle, so, if the king thought fit, he should now send to
the white eagle of the mountain for advice as to what should be
done. And the old man's counsel was thought to be good. So
a messenger was sent to the white eagle, returning after many
months during all of which time no man had dared to set foot
in the long hall of the worm.

'Upon his return the messenger declared that the white
eagle of the mountain had told him that the worm had been
sent by an evil spirit as a curse upon the people who were
happy and prosperous under Diarmid's rule and who, in con-
sequence, were envied and hated by those who were evil.
Further, that for seven years the worm would rule in King
Diarmid's castle, and that during those years the king and his
court would wander homeless through all the land. At the end
of the seventh year, however, the worm, then grown to a full-
sized dragon, would leave the castle, and though Diarmid and
his court would rule in the castle again, the dragon would rule
the land, devouring the corn, the cattle, and men, making all
desolate and leaving alone only those within the castle-walls.
Finally, that only on the last day of each seventh year would it
be possible for a brave man to kill the dragon, and so ransom
the kingdom.

'And all that the white eagle of the mountain told to the
messenger of King Diarmid came to pass. Since then, on the
last day of each seventh year the bravest man of the king's
court has tried to kill the dragon and so release the land for the
people, and gain for himself the three-fold prize. But all so far
have failed. Diarmid is long dead; many kings have succeeded
him. Today King Brude rules in the castle; but the dragon still
rules the land. And today is the last day of the seventh year;
today Morac fights the dragon.'

Borrobil quickened his pace, for with all this talking they
had fallen far behind Giric who was now well ahead.

But Donald had still one more question. 'What is the three-fold prize?' he asked.

'The king's daughter, half the kingdom, and the magic sword Greysteel, the sword that is still embedded in the yew,' answered Borrobil. 'For when Diarmid's messenger came back from the white eagle he brought with him a mighty sword, fashioned by the mountain dwarfs, a sword able to cut through iron and bronze, and its edge one that no magic spells could blunt. And this sword, acting on the instructions of the white eagle, King Diarmid drove up to its hilt in the yew tree that grows at the castle gate where he holds his court; and he gave out the promise of the white eagle, that whosoever should kill the dragon the sword should be his. But although the sword seemed to pass with ease into the trunk of the yew when King Diarmid drove it there, no man has yet been able to draw it forth and there today it still remains. No rust grows upon it, and its hilt still gleams with the jewels embedded there. Should Morac slay the dragon, the spell on the sword will enable him to draw it freely from the tree; and so, as I said, the three-fold prize will fall to him – a kingdom, a maid, and a sword. No man could wish for more. And yet even more than that will Morac gain. For, should he slay the dragon, he will also have the dragon's skin.'

Donald would now have liked to ask about the dragon's skin, but Borrobil gave him no chance. He walked on so quickly as he strove to catch up with Giric, that the two children were again hard put to it to keep near him. And by the time they had caught up with Giric the wood was far behind and they were crossing a broad stretch of marshy land. In the distance they could see a lake shimmering in the morning light; and obviously Giric was leading them straight towards it. As they drew nearer, Donald saw that an island stood in the centre of the lake and that it was crowded with buildings.

Soon they had reached the water's edge. Giric stopped, and made a signal with his hand. At once a boat pushed out from the island and drew towards them. When it had come close enough, one of the men in the boat stood up and gave a call.

Giric answered, and the boat came on again. It grounded. Giric lifted Donald and Jean into the arms of one of the rowers, Borrobil jumped aboard, and Giric followed him. Quickly the boat was rowed back to the island, and they were stepping on land again. But as Donald looked down, he saw it was not 'land' at all. Nor was the 'island' an island. Thick wooden logs had been driven down through the water, and other logs had been fastened across them to make one big wooden platform holding a village right in the centre of the lake. And all the houses of the village were built of wood, their walls being fastened to the logs that rose upright from the water.

And now the man who had stood up in the boat to call to Giric led them down a narrow 'street' (or rather down a narrow strip of the wooden platform on which no houses stood), until he stopped before a house that was larger than the rest. Here they were left outside, while their guide went in.

'You will soon see Morac now,' said Borrobil. 'He is certain to be here with King Brude.'

'And then he'll fight the dragon?' asked Donald.

'Yes.'

'But is *this* the king's house?' asked Jean. 'It doesn't look like a king's house to me.'

Jean was finding it difficult to understand the houses they had visited. First a long underground passage, cold and dark, which was apparently Giric's 'house'; and now what looked like a wooden shed on a queer wooden island in the middle of a lake, which was apparently a king's 'house'.

'No; not his proper house,' answered Borrobil. 'King Brude still has his castle which, as the white eagle foretold, the dragon can neither enter nor harm. But here King Brude has come to consult with Morac about the fight. And from here we shall go to the fight, for near by lies the dragon's hollow, on the other side of the water. This wooden island is the only place where the king's people outside his castle can live. Over all the king's *land* the dragon reigns. But once, one man fleeing from it, took to a boat and rowed out into the middle of this lake. Then did he discover to his joy that across the water the dragon could not follow him. Round and round the edge of the lake went the dragon; round and round it went until it became dizzy and all curled up in so many knots that the man escaped even while it was trying to untie itself again. And when the wise men in the castle heard of that, at once they decided to build an island in the very centre of the lake so that the people might have a place of safety in which to live. And here, apart from those in the castle, here are all those who are left of King Diarmid's once populous kingdom. A few unhappy men, women and children living on a wooden platform in a lake, occasionally venturing to the land either by boat or by the causeway which they have built in a zigzag just below the level of the water so that the dragon cannot cross by it. A people always living in fear. And all because of the dragon. May Morac win. May Giric's counsel aid him in the fight.'

This was sad and serious talking. And the children felt unhappy and subdued.

'But there is one thing I had nearly forgotten,' continued Borrobil. 'You must offer a present to the king. Have you anything you can give to him?'

Jean felt her lucky-stone in her pocket. No, she couldn't give up that. She might need it to bring her luck.

'I've got my biscuits,' said Donald, 'I could give him those.'

CHAPTER 6

The Dragon; and How Morac
Fought to Win

'I WONDER if the king will be sitting on his throne, with a crown and sceptre,' thought Jean to herself. She wasn't quite sure what a sceptre was, but she knew that it went with a crown, like a 'brush and comb' or a 'cup and saucer'. And she was saying to herself 'cup and saucer; crown and sceptre', when the curtain hanging in front of the door was pulled back, someone made a sign, and they entered the 'house'.

They found themselves in a long and narrow room completely bare of all furniture and fittings save for two wooden benches that ran down its length on either side. The low-pitched roof, so low that Donald thought he could almost touch it if he stretched up his hand, was supported on three pillars standing in line down the centre of the floor and each made of the solid trunk of a huge tree. In front of the nearest of these massive wooden uprights some six or seven men were ranged on either side of a tall white-headed man dressed in a loose leather coat covered with small rings made of bright metal. At his side hung a sword; those who stood by him held in their hands long spears with the hafts resting on the floor. But the king, for so the children guessed the white-headed man to be, wore no crown, nor, so far as Jean could see, had he anything that looked as though it could possibly be a sceptre.

'Well come, Giric,' said the king. 'And well come, Borrobil. Now we are met.'

'And here are the two children, Donald and Jean,' said Borrobil, adding in a quick whisper to Donald – 'Your present!'

Donald put his hand into his pocket, then shyly stepping forward made the best bow he could and held out his biscuits to the king. The king took the biscuits gravely.

'We are glad to welcome Borrobil's two guests,' he said, 'even though there is serious work to be done. And we are honoured by the gift.' With that he looked at the biscuits in his hand. Immediately his face changed, and a look of wonder, followed by elation, came into his eyes. He shouted aloud: 'Three! And corn upon them!' Those on either side of him cried out and clustered round. Giric actually smiled, a queer sort of twisted grin. Borrobil also smiled, a wider smile than he'd ever smiled before, if that was possible, and turning to Donald made a deep bow, deeper than any of those he'd made before, if that also was possible. Donald looked in amazement from Borrobil to the king, from the king to Giric, and from Giric to the men who were now handling his three biscuits as though they were choicest pieces of precious ware. All this was beyond him.

'A song, Borrobil!' cried the king.

Borrobil stood for a moment, thinking, then began:

> '*Nine are the stones of the Beltane Ring;*
> *Three are the gifts the children bring.*
> *Three threes are nine.*
>
> '*Nine Standing Stones where the White King wins;*
> *With threefold gift the day begins.*
> *Three threes are nine.*
>
> '*The White King wins, the Summer's born;*
> *His heralds come with triple corn.*
> *Three threes are nine.*
>
> '*A harvest rich shall crown the year;*
> *Thrice did the golden sheaves appear.*
> *Three threes are nine.*
>
> '*When the dragon rules no crop is won;*
> *The dragon's rule its course has run.*
> *Three threes are nine.*'

'Bravo!' cried everyone. For a moment, too, it looked as though everyone had forgotten Donald and Jean – everyone, that is, except Borrobil. Whispering in Donald's ear he said,

'It's wonderful! A stranger to the land brings forth the triple corn! I never knew your present was going to be anything like that. Don't you see, your three biscuits (and when you said you had your "biscuits" I'll confess the word was new to me, and I didn't quite know what you meant) – don't you see, your three biscuits with the wheatsheaves on them are a definite omen that there will be a bumper harvest this year. Three wheatsheaves! And three is the most magic number there is. But there's never been a harvest of any kind since the dragon ruled the land, driving the people to the wooden island of the lake, and penning the king in his castle. So if there *is* to be a bumper harvest this year, it can mean only one thing – that Morac will slay the dragon. It's wonderful! Now do I know why Eochaid rode in the grey light of dawn on this very day. Now do I know that the omen was good.' His eyes shone with pleasure; and again he swept the ground with his hat, in the tip of which the white owl's feather bobbed excitedly up and down.

Suddenly, the king's voice was heard above the rest. 'We forget ourselves,' he cried. 'Where are our guests?' And as the ring of men clustered around him broke apart, the king came forward to Donald and Jean.

'In our great joy at the good omens you have brought to us, to our shame we forgot for a time the bringers. You shall have the best that my land can give, though alas, it is poor enough; you shall have the freedom of my castle and hall, though alas, it is small enough; you shall sit at my side, be of my court, ride with my household, go as you will and where you will. For all the people of my afflicted land, I thank you.'

Donald blushed a deep red, and Jean's eyes sparkled. But before either of them could speak, the king turned, and in a strong voice called 'Morac!' A young man disengaged himself from the group and coming towards the children said, 'I am Morac; and I, too, would thank you. Now I know that today I shall be strong to win.' And smiling at them, he lifted his spear as though poised to strike, holding it thus while he called out three times in a loud voice, 'Morac! Morac! Morac!'

'We are ready?' asked the king.

'Ready all,' came the general shout.

There was a move to the door of the 'house', Donald and Jean finding themselves on either side of King Brude, with Morac, Giric, and Borrobil immediately behind. Outside, the people of the island seemed to have assembled in readiness and there were shouts of 'Morac!' as they passed to the waiting boats. Soon there were dozens of small boats crossing the lake, while those for whom there was no room in the boats began to make their way over the hidden causeway. All were excited; there was shouting and calling to one another. But Donald and Jean were too thrilled to do anything except watch the boats and the men, and wonder about the coming fight.

They crossed to the farther side of the lake. Here everyone quickly moved off towards a cluster of small hills in the near distance, where the children could see those in front already scrambling up the slopes and lining the low crests. But the king, with Morac and all those who had been in the king's 'house' on the island, halted at the foot of the nearest hill. And there a council was held. Donald and Jean stood outside the ring of men and could hear little of what was said; but as the talk went on they could see Giric shaking his head vigorously in disagreement. Someone handed a sword to Morac. He in turn handed his spear to one of those who stood by, and then stepping to one side brandished the sword over his head; but it shivered in splinters. A second sword was handed to him. This also he brandished over his head; and it broke in pieces. Then Giric pushed forward, and taking a long lance in his hand spoke earnestly, making many gestures with lance and hand. Morac and the king were smiling and nodding their heads. The rest of those around were obviously agreeing, too. Morac took the lance, and moving away from the group walked to a nearby tree where a boy was standing with a horse, all ready, saddled and bridled. Here he turned for a second, and, seeing the children, half-raised the lance in salute to them. Giric joined him. The Council broke up.

Borrobil came over to Donald and Jean. 'That's that,' he said; and the way he said it seemed to indicate that 'that', whatever it was, was thoroughly satisfactory. 'And now for the fight,' he continued. 'Up the hill, both of you.' And leading the way he began to climb the slope. It was an easy climb, even for Jean. Soon they were on the crest and standing beside the king. And there was the dragon!

The cluster of low hills formed a ring round a stretch of smooth turf in the hollow beneath. To Jean it looked as though they were standing on the rim of a large bowl with a bottom of green grass. But the men who had come from the island to watch the fight, the king, the king's men, Borrobil, all of them, were standing only on one side of the 'bowl'. At the other side, resting on the grass, was a large yellow head, with two wicked eyes. Every now and then the head would raise itself from the ground and move slowly from side to side. Then its mouth would open, and a greenish vapour come out and lose itself in the air. For a time, Donald found it impossible to move his eyes from that awful head. Then, as he looked, he saw that the dragon had wound its long yellowy body round and round one of the hills on the other side of the 'bowl'. It reminded him of a tug-of-war he had once seen in which the last man of each side had wound the rope round and round his waist before poising himself to act as an anchor for his side.

'It always fights like that,' whispered Borrobil. 'On the last day of every seventh year it waits here in the Dragon's Hollow, with its long body curled round the Worm's Hill. Probably the Black Eagle willed that it should wait here, so that the man who had been chosen for the fight should know where to come, and where to meet it. But although all so far have fallen before it in the fight, Giric has a plan. Morac *will* win.' And Borrobil, though his voice was serious, actually smiled his old merry smile.

Jean clutched him tightly with one hand; in the other, she clutched equally tightly her lucky-stone.

'Oh! but it *is* geesty,' she whispered. 'I don't want to stay. Can't we go back, Borrobil?'

Donald, too, began to think that a dragon-fight was far different from all that he had pictured it to be. But if both of them were afraid, it was not for themselves they were afraid, it was for Morac.

Yet even before Borrobil could answer, a shout echoed from the men around, and there, through a gap between the hills, came Morac, riding into the hollow. 'Whatever has he got?' thought Donald to himself. And then he saw. Morac was carrying the long lance that Giric had handed to him, and on its point was a ball of burning fire. He reined in his horse, and then, setting his lance in rest, rode furiously, straight for the dragon's head. The monster raised its head from the ground to meet him; it belched forth its green and poisonous breath. But the lance was long; the deadly breath did not reach far enough; and down into the yawning mouth went the ball of fire on the point of Morac's lance. Down into the dragon's mouth; down into its throat; down; deep down; and the lance broke. The horse was jerked back on its haunches, almost unseating Morac. But immediately regaining his balance, he turned round and rode back a short distance, then turned again to face the dragon's head.

And now came a dreadful sight. Part of the broken lance could be seen sticking out from the monster's mouth. But instead of a poisonous green breath, now the dragon breathed forth smoke and flames; instead of the awful head moving slowly from side to side with baleful glance, now it moved round and round in fast wide circles, and now to and fro (just as a dog would worry a rat, thought Donald to himself), ever and always striving to rid itself of lance and burning fire. Yet the fire within the dragon's throat grew no less. Tongues of flame and clouds of black smoke poured forth. Now the lashings of the head grew less wide, less violent. The head sank lower and lower; the wicked eyes grew glazed and dim.

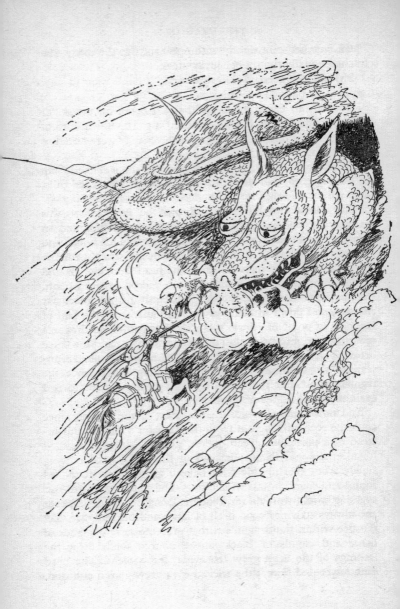

Had the dragon met its end at last? No! Again the head lashed fearfully about. And this time Donald, gazing with fascinated eyes, could see the long body round the hill draw its folds tighter and tighter, until he thought the hill would crack. But it was the last spasm. Suddenly the long body relaxed; the head sank down upon the ground, smoke and flames still issuing from its mouth; the eyes closed. Once more they opened. They closed. Closed they remained. The dragon was dead! A cry was heard in the heavens, and a black eagle could be seen soaring high amid the clouds. The dragon was dead! The curse was lifted from the land!

There was a long silence, broken by a great roar from the assembled host, the king's shout being the loudest of all. Men could be seen seizing each other by the hand; some even wept in their joy. Many began to run down the hill towards the hollow beneath. Soon all were running to the farther side, all except the king and those immediately around him, and except Borrobil and the children. Somehow, neither Donald nor Jean felt inclined to approach that awful monster, dead though it was; and Borrobil, sensing this, stayed with them. From their place on the hill they could see the crowd surging down; but they also saw something else. Long before those rushing across the hollow could reach the long yellow body of the dead dragon, they saw Morac step quickly to the head, where, taking a knife, or a short sword, he cut something away, put it to his lips and then cast it aside. They heard Borrobil murmur

> *'So now the future's weal or woe*
> *Shall Morac see and Morac know.'*

Donald turned to him. 'What did you say?' he asked.

Borrobil looked at him. 'Morac has been the first to touch with his lips the dragon's skin,' he said, 'and with that touch he has gained the "second-sight", a sight into the future, so that now from time to time he will be able to tell what lies ahead – a ship that will not return; a death that awaits a man; a battle lost or won. Not always will the second-sight come to him, but at times he will find himself seeing ahead, and knowing the future and what it holds. It is magic I would have dearly liked myself.'

'But, please, Borrobil, what was the ball of fire which Morac used to kill the dragon?' asked Jean.

'Ah,' he answered, 'that was Giric's plan. Always in the past the dragon has won the fight because its poisonous breath has reached out to kill, so preventing brave men with sword and shield from approaching near enough to strike even one sure blow. Many times had Giric seen that happen. And yet a lance would not suffice, for once it had pierced the dragon the bearer of the lance would be within reach of the dragon's breath; he would be killed forthwith and so would be unable to continue the fight. But following the counsel Giric gave to him, Morac fastened to the point of his lance a peat dipped in strongest pitch. Setting this alight, he drove it, as you saw, deep down the dragon's throat. The blazing pitch with its smoke and smell overcame the poisonous vapour of the dragon's breath; Morac could drive down his lance and still live. More than that, the blazing pitch with running fire ran down the dragon's throat, deep into its vital parts, making doubly fatal the lance's wound. It was a cunning plan, and boldly was it carried out.'

Once more the children looked across to the dragon's lair. Around Morac they could see a swaying crowd of men, but already the crowd was breaking up. Many men were now hacking at the long body curled around the hill; large pieces were being cut off it and cast into a great fire. Morac was beginning to make his way across the hollow. He came to the foot of the hill where King Brude was standing with his men and where, above them, Borrobil stood with Donald and Jean.

Morac approached the king and knelt on one knee. But the king spoke quickly: 'Rise, Morac,' he said. 'Already you are my son. And when the time shall come for me to go, you in turn shall be king of this land. And a land that shall again be blessed by plenty and happiness. Forthwith you shall ride with the good news to the North, and thence bring back Finella, my daughter, so that you may be wed in my own castle, with the blessings of all my people upon you. But before you ride there is the sword Greysteel, waiting to be drawn from the yew, the sword that is yours of right. Come then, and bring with you the stranger children who appeared with Borrobil, for to them also is much honour due.'

The king moved away with his men. Morac ran lightly up the slope and seizing a hand of each of the children cried out 'And so the dragon's course has run! And all your omens were true. How can I thank you; and how can I thank Giric? You will bring them to the castle, won't you Borrobil? You'd like to come, both of you, wouldn't you?'

'Yes, rather!' cried Donald, while Jean, looking at him with bright eyes said 'Oh, that *was* a rumpledy knock you gave the dragon.'

Morac laughed. 'Come on,' he said. 'I'll give you both a ride; one in front and one behind. We can ride at a walk and we shall be there as soon as the others. Also Borrobil can walk beside us. It won't wear out his legs.' And he grinned cheerfully.

With Morac they ran down to the level grass where he had left his horse. He mounted, and then, leaning over, lifted first Donald to sit behind him with his arms round his waist, and then Jean to sit in front and to hold on to the horse's mane. In this way they rode slowly out of the hollow and across the heath beyond.

Soon they had reached Brude's castle, the castle where, in Diarmid's day, the Black Eagle had first left the accursèd egg. Just inside the castle-gate, they could see the king, and with him many others, standing by a dark green tree. They rode up to the group, and Morac, lifting down the children – first Jean and then Donald – dismounted from his horse. The crowd in front of the tree parted, leaving a path, along which Morac walked until he stood by the king beneath the overhanging branches of the yew. Donald and Jean had followed him, so that they, too, were under the tree and in the very front of the crowd. And there, in the thick heart of the yew tree's trunk they could see the hilt of a sword, with many jewels in it, flashing with rays of light. So brightly shone that jewelled hilt, that the sword might have been driven into the tree only yesterday; but it had been there more years than many a man could tell, waiting to be drawn by the hand that slew the dragon.

Morac paused for a while. Then, stretching out his hand he grasped firmly the jewelled hilt and drew. The sword came out of the yew as easily as ever came sword from scabbard, and, as it came, there was a sound of music, light and rippling, like the cadence of a brook in summer dancing over the stones in its path. Morac lifted the sword high above his head. It flashed like summer lightning. He brandished it. Again it sang, but now like the wind in a gale that bends tall trees in its wake. He held it before him, and his face shone in the light reflected from the magic metal of the dwarfs. 'May I never wield thee save in causes that are true and just and honourable,' he said; and as he spoke, again the sword sang and now its music was like the deep note of thunder rolling in the far-off hills.

All had stood spell-bound. All tongues were tied. But now the silence was broken by the king. 'A song!' he called, 'Borrobil! A song!' Borrobil came up to where Morac stood with the magic sword in his hand. He seemed to bow to it, and then began

> '*I sing of Morac!*
> *Morac the dragon slew;*
> *Morac the sword withdrew*
> *Forth from the darkling yew.*
> *Hail to thee Morac!*
>
> '*I sing of Morac!*
> *Now shall he journey far,*
> *His guide the northern star;*
> *Nought shall his right debar*
> *To fair Finella.*
>
> '*I sing of Morac!*
> *Fast may he come again;*
> *Fast bringing in his train*
> *His bridal queen to reign*
> *The fair Finella.*
>
> '*I sing of Morac!*
> *Morac, the magic brand*
> *Morac, the princess' hand*
> *Morac, our own proud land*
> *Long may he treasure!*'

Borrobil ended, and all greeted his song with shouts of approval.

'So be it,' added the king gravely. 'When shall you fare forth, Morac; shall it be forthwith, or shall you wait awhile?'

'I go forthwith,' he answered, and there was eagerness in his voice. 'Giric shall come with me to act as guide. Borrobil also shall come, if he is of a mind.'

'May I come, too?' said Jean in a still small voice.

Morac smiled, and the king, turning to her, patted her on the head. 'Do you really want to go?' he said. 'There may be dangers. Though after all we could probably find a horse small enough for you.'

'Ah! but', answered Jean, 'Morac has a magic sword. And if Borrobil goes I shan't know what to do betil he returns; for I don't know anybody besept you and Morac and Giric and Borrobil.'

The king turned to Borrobil and spoke to him in a whisper. At first Borrobil shook his head. They talked together still more. And in the end Borrobil seemed to agree. 'Right then,' said the king. 'Donald and Jean shall each have a horse and they shall ride with Morac and Giric. I gave my word that they should ride where they would and as they would. That word I keep. But in your care, Morac, shall they be: for Borrobil must stay with me a while; I have other work for him to do.'

Morac was already mounted on the horse that had carried him in his fight with the dragon. Giric, too, was astride a horse. And now one of the king's men led out for the children two small and shaggy ponies which seemed very quiet, very tame, just the right height, and very happy to be setting forth. There were shouts of farewell; Borrobil came running up to the children, with his old merry smile, telling them that soon he would be seeing them once more, and waving his funny hat with the white owl's feather in its tip. So did they ride out of the castle-gate and on their way to the north.

As they passed the low cluster of hills by the dragon's hollow, no longer was a long yellow body curled round and round the Worm's Hill. All of it had been cut to pieces and thrown into the large fire which still blazed fiercely near by. But all round the hill Donald could see sharp ridges in the grass where the dragon had tightened its body in that last convulsive movement when he had thought the hill would crack. 'Now I know what makes those ridges on the sides of hills,' he said to himself; 'but what a lot of dragons must have been killed all over the country in the days gone by.'

CHAPTER 7

Caught in the Mist

THEIR way lay across the heath and then up the deep valley of a small but fast-running stream. Giric, as their guide, rode ahead, followed by Morac with Donald and Jean. From time to time the track in the river-valley narrowed and they were compelled to ride in single file. Then Morac would bring up the rear with Donald and Jean riding ahead of him. Once, when they were riding in this way in single file, Donald thought of the riddle of the number of eggs in the old woman's basket – 'one before two; one behind two; one between two'. He tried to work out how that riddle could be asked when there were four of them instead of three. But in the end he gave it up.

For a long time they rode in silence. Also, both the children were at first much too concerned with getting the 'feel' of their shaggy ponies to want to talk. But gradually they began to get their 'balance' and to grow accustomed to their new 'seats'.

'Are we going to meet a *real* princess?' asked Jean.

'Yes,' replied Morac. 'We go to bring back the Princess Finella, who will be my bride. Long have we loved one another; and perhaps because of that, King Brude and his council agreed that next on the last day of the seventh year the turn should be mine to face the dragon and to try to win the three-fold prize. Only the Black Sulig opposed it. But he could name no other in my place; and by all men is he feared and distrusted.'

'And will the Princess have a golden crown and a lovely dress?' continued Jean, who felt that King Brude, at any rate, had been sadly wanting in having neither crown nor sceptre.

'No, no,' answered Morac, laughing. 'She will be dressed in plain and simple clothes. Here, since the dragon ruled, we have had no fine dress, no gold nor ornament; for such things are the things of plenty and peace. But now that the dragon is dead, the land will flourish again. King Brude will wear his crown; and the Princess Finella shall be radiant in rich apparel.'

Jean paused awhile, and then said gravely, 'I think that sounds nice.'

'So do I,' laughed Morac.

'Ah! but you are going to marry the princess,' was Jean's reply.

Again Morac laughed. And now Donald broke in:

'But where *is* Finella? Where shall we find her? Is it far?'

'Not very far,' answered Morac. 'Once we have passed the forest in which Black Sulig's castle is hidden, we shall soon be there. But seven years ago, when last the dragon was fought in vain, King Brude, fearing for Finella's safety, and sad at the thought of her constant imprisonment within the castle-walls, sent her to the Men of Orc – a noble race holding the kingdom adjacent to his own. And with them has she stayed ever since, in one of their strange but strong castles, which you shall see yourselves. How long it will take us to reach their kingdom I cannot say; but you will know it as soon as we come there, for nowhere else have I seen castles like those that are built by the Men of Orc; and in the very largest of them lives Finella.'

'Why, what are they like?' asked Donald.

'You shall see for yourself,' said Morac, with a smile. 'It shall be a surprise for you.'

'Well then,' persisted Donald, 'who is Black Sulig? Why is his castle hidden in a forest? Does no one know where to find it?'

Morac looked at Donald without speaking. He seemed to be thinking what to say. 'Sulig,' he said at last, 'is a magician; yet also is he a member of the council of the king. Many are afraid of him; all men hate him. And yet King Brude suffers him to attend his councils, listens to his word, and treats him as he treats all others. For although there are stories of his wickedness – stories of a magic which is black magic, far different from the magic of Borrobil – they are still stories and nothing more. Yet I believe that should proof of his evil and wickedness ever come to the king, at once King Brude would order him to be put to death. But Brude is of all kings the most just. And of the Black Sulig there are many stories but no proof.'

Donald digested this in silence. 'I expect he has hidden his castle in the forest so that no one will see his black magic and how he does it,' he said at last.

'I cannot say,' answered Morac slowly. 'I have never seen the Sulig's castle, nor have I met any man who has set eyes upon it. Again there are stories but no proof. It is said to be hidden in the forest. It is said to have been built by magic upon pillars of sand with chaff for their mortar. It is said that Sulig has enchained a spirit there that tells him the future and things that happen afar off. It is said that should Sulig die, his castle will fall; for the pillars of sand, held together by his black magic, will crumble at his death. It is said . . . but many things are *said*, and of proof there is none.'

At this point their path narrowed again, so that Morac had to drop behind and once more they were riding in single file. And now the path seemed to grow narrower and narrower as they made their way up the valley of the stream. Now, too, on either side of them rose thickly-wooded hills, which darkened the valley and seemed to shut them in. Far ahead all they could see was still a narrow valley and still a black mass of trees on either side. Soon the children could not help thinking of their first journey to the wood, when all this strange adventure had begun. The narrow valley between the dark woods was strangely like that dark and narrow lane which they had climbed to reach the Eldritch Wood and the Nine-Stone-Ring. Soon, too, they began to feel that the four of them were far too few, and that they were small and helpless in a doubtful land. Then they remembered Morac's magic sword and took courage again. But it was only for a while, and again the feeling of helplessness would return and weigh them down.

In the half-light of the valley, made dim by the woods above, their progress seemed to grow slower and slower. There were many twists and turns, as the fast-running stream itself twisted and turned; there were large rocks which made the path wind first this way, then that. And then, suddenly, they found themselves in a thick white mist which seemed to fold itself round them on all sides at once, and which cut them off from one another, so that each of them now rode alone. Donald heard Giric call out, but the sound of Giric's voice might have come from any direction – from the right, or the left, from behind him, or from in front of him. His pony had stopped, and wisely he knew that if he stayed still, Morac, riding behind, would be

sure to come up to him simply by following the path. But even as this thought was passing through his mind, he felt himself lifted out of the saddle and carried up into the air. He tried to call out but found he could make no sound. It seemed as though far below him he heard shouting; but the confused noise soon died away and he remembered nothing more.

And shouting there certainly had been. As soon as the mist had descended upon them, Morac had ridden quickly forward, only to find Donald's and Jean's ponies standing quietly side by side, with their saddles empty, and Donald and Jean nowhere to be seen. Giric had ridden back and joined him. Together they had called out, making the valley echo and re-echo with their calls; but there had come no answer. Then, as quickly as it had descended upon them, the mist began to thin and to disappear.

'Sulig!' cried Giric.

'True!' answered Morac, and drew his sword. But as the blade came forth it gave a sound like a low moan, and Morac knew that its magic was of no avail. In despair they looked at one another; and somewhere from the thinning mist above they heard a low and cunning laugh.

'Yes, Sulig,' continued Morac in a strange voice. 'But now I see him lying crushed and broken like an adder trodden under a man's heel.' He shook himself, and looked at Giric, and a queer light was dancing in his eyes. 'Giric,' he said slowly, 'I have felt for the first time the power that I gained from the dragon's skin, and in the "second sight" have I seen the Black Sulig dead.'

CHAPTER 8

Prisoners of Sulig

DONALD rubbed his eyes. Had he been asleep? When did he go to bed? Somehow he couldn't remember that! Then, with a rush, he remembered the ride up the narrow valley with Morac and Giric, the sudden mist, and how he had been lifted up into the air. He sat up quickly with the thought 'Where is Jean?' But his fear for her subsided at once, for there she was, lying just beside him and apparently still fast asleep.

'Jean! Jean!' he called. 'Wake up! I want to talk to you.' He pulled her by the shoulder. Jean muttered something to herself and tried to turn over. She felt for the accustomed blankets. They were not there! That was funny! She opened her eyes and saw Donald leaning over her excitedly.

'Oh! I do wish you wouldn't distrumple me so,' she complained.

'I didn't,' Donald began, then stopped. There was a moment's pause before he spoke again, this time quietly and anxiously. 'Jean,' he said, 'I don't know where we are, but I think we've been taken prisoner. Do you remember that mist? I expect you were lifted up, too. We've been taken from Morac and Giric.'

His words roused Jean far sooner than anything else could have done. She sat up and wrinkled her forehead and the top of her nose. 'I was belifted from my horse,' she said slowly, 'and then I can't remember what happened after that. But won't Morac come for us?'

Donald didn't answer her. He looked round for the first time. They were lying on a rough carpet of grass or rushes, spread over the stone floor of a small room. The walls, too, were of stone; and high up in one wall was a narrow slit through which came a little light. But there seemed to be no door. He turned to look at Jean sitting up beside him, and saw that she, too, must have been looking round the room for now her lower lip was beginning to quiver and her eyes were beginning to fill. 'Don't cry, Jean,' he said gently. 'I know we shan't be here long. Morac and Borrobil and King Brude will soon find out that we've been carried away. Why, Morac must know already!'

'But I can't help crying when I'm unhappy,' sobbed Jean. 'And I shan't be happy again betil Morac or Borrobil finds us.'

Donald put his arm round Jean's shoulders and once more looked round the room. That narrow slit in the wall was too high for him to reach. And what could he do even if somehow or other he could manage to reach it? But where *was* the door? They must have come through a door to get into the room, and yet there was no door to be seen. He took his arm from Jean's shoulders and stood up. Four walls, but no door. That was nonsense. He walked round the walls, examining each one carefully for its whole length. Somewhere he had read of secret doors that could be found by tapping the walls. He began to knock one wall with his fist, but the rough stonework hurt; and in any case, he thought, I shouldn't know what sort of sound a secret door would make. He sat down again on the floor. What could he do? There must be something he could do! They were shut in. No, they were walled in. Had they been walled in for ever? Were they to be left here to starve? No! That was silly. Besides he must think of a way out. There must be some way out.

Once more he looked round; once more he shrank back at the sight of those four bare walls. But by now Jean had recovered from her first fright.

'I think Morac will kill somebody with his magic sword when he finds out who has put us in here,' she said, confidently. 'And it's a big sword, and Morac is a brave man. We'd just better wait here, for I've still got my lucky-stone.' And she held out her round yellow pebble for Donald to see.

'Yes,' he agreed doubtfully. 'If Morac can find us.'

'Well, if Morac can't, Borrobil can. For Borrobil's a

magician. Perhaps Borrobil will find us and then perhaps
Morac will be able to kill somebody.'

'*Perhaps*,' said a nasty voice.

Both of them jumped. In the far corner of the room a square
piece of the floor stood up like the lid of a box. In the opening
was a head, the neck just level with the floor, so that for a
moment Donald thought it was a head only, a head without a
body, and yet a head that spoke.

'Come,' the head said; and it was not a nice head either. It
was thick and broad, with a mop of untidy red hair hanging
down over the eyes which were sly and cruel. At its bidding
Jean shrank back, and for a second Donald wondered whether
he could bang that uplifted door hard back again on to that
nasty looking head. But what would he do then?

'Come,' the head repeated.

They saw that they could do nothing but obey. They got up
slowly and reluctantly, and moved towards the opening in the
floor. The head disappeared. And now they saw that a flight
of stone steps led downwards. Donald went first with Jean
following him. The steps were short but steep, and brought
them to a passage in which, ahead of them, they saw the
grotesque figure of a dwarf. His head, which they recognized
as that which had spoken to them from the floor of the room,
seemed almost as big as his body; his legs were so small that
they looked bound to break beneath his weight. But, and of
major importance, he carried over his shoulder a large and
knobbly club. Despite his small legs the dwarf moved surprisingly fast. Every now and then he would turn round to see that
the children were following, then he would shake his club
threateningly, and move on again. 'He might know we are
following him,' thought Donald to himself. 'Where else could
we go anyway?' Strangely enough, he felt no fear, and Jean
had apparently lost all her fear too, for once, when the dwarf
turned round and shook his knobbly club at them, she whispered to Donald, 'Morac's sword is better than a big club,
anyway.'

Unexpectedly the passage came to a dead-end. Donald was

beginning to wonder what would happen next, when the dwarf seized hold of an iron ring in the wall and pulled. A large stone swung to one side, and again there was a flight of steps, but this time leading upwards. And this time the dwarf pointed to the steps with his club, indicating that now they were to go ahead of him. As they climbed the steps they heard a dull thud behind them. They looked down. The stone had swung back into its place and the dwarf was no longer with them. 'I'm glad he's gone,' said Jean simply, 'though I wasn't befrightened very much of his club.' And the thought that the dwarf had left them seemed to make it easier to climb the remaining steps and to meet what lay ahead.

A few more steps, and they had entered a long hall, dimly lit by the uncertain light that came through a series of small windows high above the stone arches of the walls. To this dim light was added the glow from two braziers burning red at the farther end of the hall; and between and slightly in front of the braziers, so that at first he appeared only as a dark silhouette, stood a man, apparently waiting for them. The man walked slowly towards them, and as he drew near, at once they knew him. He was the Black Sulig! There could be no mistake. The swarthy face, with its thick black beard, the heavy black eyebrows, the mass of long black hair – all fully explained that name. His eyes, too, were jet black, bright and piercing, and as he looked searchingly at the children those eyes seemed to go right through them as though reading their very minds. Involuntarily Donald looked away, and as he did so his glance fell on a heavy chest, made of some dark wood bound with iron, standing in a corner and revealed by the glow from the burning braziers. 'Jewels, perhaps,' flashed through his mind, 'stolen, I expect'; and then he felt his eyes being drawn back again to the Black Sulig.

'So you are Donald and Jean.' The voice to their surprise was smooth and almost pleasant.

'Yes,' answered Donald. 'We . . .' Somehow he felt he ought to say something more; he ought to protest at their capture; but try as he would the right words would not come.

'So!' and a note of triumph crept into the man's voice. 'So! I have planned well. Now in Brude's court and council shall Morac be despised of all. Morac who slew the dragon; Morac who won the sword Greysteel; Morac who is to wed the fair Finella. Morac the hero; Morac the great. Now shall this marvellous Morac be laughed at and shunned. The brave Morac with his magic sword who still failed to guard two

children in the pass. So! I am more than content. For I, Black Sulig, hold the stranger children. Morac – even King Brude himself – shall plead with me for you. I shall hide you where no man can find you. And they shall plead with me. Then will I ask for . . . What? What shall I ask for you? That Morac be banished? That Morac give me the magic sword Greysteel in exchange for you? That might be worth while, but would it be enough? What shall I ask for you? You shall see.'

To the children's surprise he walked over to the iron-bound chest and standing in front of it spoke to it – 'What shall I ask for the stranger children? Answer me.'

'Nothing,' replied a hollow voice from the chest.

The children jumped. Their eyes widened in astonishment. But Sulig's eyes grew black with anger.

'Nothing! I shall ask nothing?'

'Nothing,' was the reply from the chest.

Sulig paused; then his face lightened.

'Fool that I am!' he cried. 'I understand. I shall ask for nothing, for much will be offered to me without the asking. I shall not need to ask.'

'Ah! but perhaps you *will* ask, and still get nothing,' interrupted Jean.

'Silence,' he roared. 'Shall a child correct me?' Yet Jean's words had touched him. He turned once more towards the chest, then stopped, and bending his piercing eyes on Jean said, 'And so you think that? Now we shall see. The spirit I have imprisoned within this chest has never failed me. And what, think you, would the wise Borrobil give for a chest such as this? I ask and it answers. I say to it, "Where are the stranger children from the court of King Brude?" It answers, "In the pass." I ask, "And who is with them?" It answers, "Morac and Giric." What would your friend Borrobil give for that? How easy for me to cover you with a mist and to carry you here! Yes! We will see what King Brude will offer for your safe return; we will see what shall be offered without my asking.'

Again he turned to the chest: 'What offers King Brude for the stranger children? Answer me.' 'Nothing,' came the hollow-voiced reply.

Once more anger seized the Black Sulig. He gripped the chest as if he would break it with his hands, and his voice rose to a shout.

'Then who shall pay their ransom?'

'No one.'

'No one!' cried Sulig. 'No one! But stay! There are two

answers to that! *Nothing* is given for the dead. *No one* ransoms the dead. Is that the way it shall be?' He smiled as if a new thought had come to him; and he looked at the children in a way that made their blood run cold, while their hearts seemed to stop beating.

Then, suddenly, the chest spoke again, and this time of its own accord. But now, instead of a low and hollow voice there came a cry, sharp and clear, with the one word 'Beware!'

There was a frantic knocking on the lid; it lifted; it half-opened; then it fell back again with a crash, followed by a faint sound like a sigh of despair. Jean was terrified; she flung her arms round Donald, and Donald's heart pounded and thumped as though it would break through his breast. Even the Black Sulig leapt back. His eyes glanced quickly round the hall. There was no one there. Only the leathern thong that served for a handle to a massive oak door in one of the arches in the wall moved slightly, to and fro, as though someone had brushed by it. As if ashamed of his momentary fear, Sulig drew himself up and laughed aloud. 'Beware!' he laughed. 'Why, indeed? Of whom, of what shall the Black Sulig beware?' He paused, and in that pause, as if in echo to his words, there came the answer:

> *'Why and what and when and where?*
> *The answer's still the same – Beware!'*

'Borrobil!' cried both the children at once, and swung round. There he stood, grinning his usual merry smile.

'At your service,' he said cheerfully. Then, in a sharper voice, 'At *your* service, too, Sulig.' And he walked towards Sulig across the floor of the hall.

CHAPTER 9

Trial by Magic

FOR a time Sulig and Borrobil stood facing one another. The contrast was more than one between a strong man in his prime and a man old in years and wisdom; it was one between evil and good. For Sulig's brow was blacker still as anger deepened it, and evil could be read in his face. At last he spoke – 'So we meet again.'

'Yes,' answered Borrobil. 'Perhaps for the last time.'

Sulig laughed. 'That sounds good to me. I have long wished that these parts were rid of an old humbug with his foolish tales, his doggerel songs, and his childish tricks.'

'But perhaps the old humbug may be able to do more than that,' replied Borrobil quietly. 'I would warn you that when the strong man lifts a feather it must not be thought he has lost his strength to lift a tree.'

'What!' cried Sulig. 'Would you put your simple petty tricks against magic such as mine?'

'Willingly,' answered Borrobil.

Sulig's eyes flashed. 'Good! Let it be so! We shall strive one against the other. Should your magic prevail over mine, the children shall be yours. But should my own magic prevail, then for ever you leave the service of King Brude, for ever you become my slave even as the spirit that I have enchained within this chest.'

'That is agreed, and more,' was Borrobil's reply.

'To the test then!' shouted Sulig. 'To the test! Out! We will go outside the castle-gate and there shall we see what the great Borrobil can do.'

Borrobil smiled and beckoned the children to his side. Then, with the Black Sulig leading the way, they passed out of the hall and so through many passages and rooms to the courtyard, and across the courtyard to the gate. At a word from Sulig the gate opened before them; at another word the heavy drawbridge dropped slowly into place. Proud in this first display of magic power, Sulig strode across the drawbridge and awaited them on the other side, standing before the tall trees of the forest that rose around his castle. 'Now let us see what the good magician can do,' he said contemptuously.

'The offer of a test was yours,' answered Borrobil. 'Put forth your power, Sulig, and it shall be answered.'

Sulig looked at him and paused. Then with a smile, he reached out his hand and made a sign. At once the trees of the forest disappeared; where they had stood, now there stretched fertile meadows and green valleys as far as the eye could reach. Donald and Jean stared open-eyed at the sudden change. Could all this have actually happened? But Borrobil merely nodded. Stepping slightly forward he spoke in a strange tongue, and his words sounded soft and persuasive like the wind sighing in the trees. Swiftly the valleys closed in, swiftly the vast expanse of green changed colour, and now all that the children saw before them was an arid desert of yellow sand.

'Too easy!' cried Sulig. 'The test must be harder yet.' Once more he reached out his hand and made a sign. And now the desert changed to an open sea. The children found themselves standing on a shingle beach; waves were gently lapping at their feet; and in the distance stately ships under full sail were moving through the waters.

Sulig turned to Borrobil and his look seemed to say, 'Now, what is your answer to that?' But again Borrobil merely nodded. Again he spoke in a strange tongue. And this time his words sounded sibilant like the wildly driving rain of the bursting cloud. Instinctively the children stepped back, and even as they moved, the sky darkened, a wind rose, the sea became a mass of wild and angry waves, and the ships, tossed hither and thither, plunged beneath the waters and were lost.

'Enough,' said Sulig bitterly. 'Prospects that are fair but false are too easily shown to be as false as once they appeared to be fair. I must try you with magic of another kind.' And

saying this he made another sign; the forest reappeared and
the children saw once more the trees, the castle-walls, and behind them the castle-gate.

Borrobil looked closely at him. 'To your other magic, then,'
he said. 'I have seen no mighty magic yet.'

Sulig made no answer, but plunging into the trees he led them down a narrow path that brought them to a wide clearing within the wood. Here he stepped alone into the middle of the clearing; here he turned to look at them, to see that they were watching him; then holding high one hand above his head, he sank slowly into the ground which closed at last above that one uplifted hand. Donald glanced at Borrobil. He saw a smile hovering round the corners of the little man's mouth and eyes. But almost at once he jumped back with a cry, for coming out of the ground immediately beside him was Sulig! Soon the Black Sulig's feet came to the level of the green grass; there he seemed to take one short step upwards, and then he was walking forward towards Borrobil.

'Perhaps your good magic can do that?' he said triumphantly. 'Can *you* descend into the ground, travel under the earth to whatever place you may desire, and then rise up again out of the earth at your journey's end? Let that be the first test in the final trial of your power and mine.'

Borrobil moved uneasily from one foot to the other. He looked strangely downcast. Donald watched him apprehensively, and a new fear struck him, a fear he had never known before. What if Borrobil should fail? Instinctively he stepped to Jean's side and reached out to hold her hand.

For what seemed to the children a long long time Borrobil was silent. Then, looking at Sulig, he said, 'That magic is indeed mighty; if, as you say, magic it is. But I saw that you yourself chose the place for your descent and the place for your return. Trickery there may be. I know not. Perhaps there is some passage between the two places that were chosen by you, a passage known to you but hidden from others. But *here*' (and Borrobil walked forward for some distance and dug his heel into the ground) 'here I challenge you to descend into the depths of the earth, to speak to me from the depths, and then to rise again from out the earth by yonder tree' (and he pointed to a tall ash on the further side of the clearing in which they stood).

Sulig lifted his black head and laughed loud and long. 'Ha!

Ha! So Borrobil begins to doubt his powers at last! Some passage below the ground! Ha! Ha!' And his disdainful laugh rang through the trees – Ha! Ha!; Ha! Ha! 'Come. You shall witness my power again. Even from the very spot you chose. Here it was, was it not?' And he stood on the place where Borrobil had dug his heel into the ground. For a moment he stood there. Then the earth seemed to open beneath him and he sank slowly out of sight. Borrobil waited for a short time, then, bending down, he called out in a shaking voice, 'Sulig! Are you indeed deep down?'

'Aye, fathoms deep,' came a muffled answer from beneath the seemingly solid earth.

'Then *stay* deep down,' cried Borrobil in his old familiar voice. '*Stay* fathoms deep.' And he spoke two words that sounded sharp and commanding, like the crack of the whip when oxen are driven at the plough. He turned to the children with a merry chuckle. 'That will teach him to go worm-hunting. But we must be off. My magic can keep him there only for a time. We must find Morac and Giric and then we can settle his account for ever.' And taking hold of the children's hands he walked them quickly across the clearing and into the shelter of the trees.

CHAPTER 10

How Borrobil Saw All that Happened; How he Made himself Invisible; and How he Reached his Journey's End as Soon as he Set Out

IN amongst the trees they were compelled to walk behind one another, but always Borrobil in front seemed to know which way to turn, which track to follow and which to avoid. Donald remembered what Borrobil had said before about knowing every path and every way, and he wondered if it was all part of his magic knowledge. 'How useful it would be in a strange town,' he thought. 'I should know at once where to find the post office, the chemist's shop, and everything else without having to ask anyone the way.'

Still they pushed on, this way and that. Soon the children were quite out of breath, and when it seemed to Jean that she could go not one step farther, she stopped and called out appealingly to Borrobil, 'Stop! Wait for me! I'm all breathed out.'

'Just one bit more,' he called back. 'We're almost there. Tell your legs we're nearly there, Jean, and see if that will help.'

Jean thought that that was just nonsense; but she struggled on again. And sure enough, when they had turned their next sharp corner the trees began to thin out and they found themselves on the edge of the forest.

Borrobil waited for them to get their breath. He had fairly rushed them through the trees and poor Jean was panting 'like a grand-puff', she said.

'That's that,' he exclaimed. 'I wanted to get out of the forest as soon as we could in order to find Morac and Giric while Sulig is still underground. Yes, I can still see him there'; and as he spoke the last words a distant look came into his eyes.

'Still *see* him there!' cried the children together.

'Yes, he's still beneath the ground,' answered Borrobil. 'Not for nothing did I rub the serpent's grease on my eyes.'

'Oh, Borrobil, you are just being silly,' said Jean.

Borrobil turned to look at her, his eyes twinkling and yet serious. 'But it's true, Jean. If you rub serpent's grease on your eyes you can see all that is happening a long way off – even on the other side of a mountain, or even, as now, in the middle of a thick forest. And that,' he continued in a graver tone, 'that is why King Brude would not let me ride with you when you left his castle to bring back the princess Finella. For Brude had long heard tales of Sulig, but always were they tales without proof. Brude likewise knew that Sulig would be jealous of Morac, and might try to do some evil to him as he rode near the forest castle, on his way through the pass. So the king bade me stay behind: thereby lulling Sulig into the belief that he would find it easy to work his will; but also knowing that Borrobil would watch you as you went, would watch you every bit of your way. And so I did. Scarcely had you ridden from the castle than I had rubbed the serpent's grease on my eyes. So did I watch you in your journey up the pass; so did I see Sulig's mist envelop you; so did I see him lift you from your saddles and carry you to his castle in the forest. Then, quickly making my way to Brude's chamber I related all that I had seen. The king had no fear for your safety; nor, indeed, had I. We knew that Sulig would not harm you but would try to hold you as hostages – perhaps for the magic sword Greysteel to be given to him in return for you. Yet Brude still told me to make what haste I could to rescue you, at the same time bidding me tell Morac that Sulig must die. The rest was easy. With fern-seed I made myself invisible; and on Hattock's Horse I made my way in less than no time to Sulig's castle, there to stand beside you in his hall.'

'And does fern-seed really make you invisible?' asked Donald, while Jean tugged at his coat to ask him what 'invisible' meant.

'Certainly it does,' answered Borrobil, 'though I nearly gave myself away when the leather thong on the door into Sulig's hall swung to and fro after I had slipped through. That sort of thing must be watched when one is moving about invisibly. And it is so easy to forget. The only real difficulty with fern-seed is in the gathering of it. That is where the trouble comes in. Many a man has set forth on the right night under the right moon, and after filling his bag with the precious seed has reached home only to find his bag as empty as when he set forth. For not only must the place and the night and the moon be right for the gathering, but also must you be absolutely sure that the fairies won't rob you of your seed as fast as you gather it into your bag. And that means speaking the right words to the fairies all the time you are gathering the seed; and the right words take many years to learn.'

'But where is your horse now?' asked Jean.

'Horse?' repeated Borrobil.

'Yes. You said you rode to Sulig's castle on somebody's horse. I heard you say so.'

Borrobil laughed. 'True. I said I rode on Hattock's Horse, but that is something quite different.'

Jean looked puzzled. 'Now you're teasing me again,' she said. Borrobil was immediately contrite. 'Oh, dear, I am sorry, really sorry,' he said. 'I keep forgetting that you cannot possibly know all the things I expect you to know. And it's sometimes so difficult to remember that. But you see, if you know the fairies well, really well, you can join them as they ride through the sky and so arrive where you want to be almost as soon as you set out. All you need to do is to cry out, "Horse and Hattock," and the fairies will carry you up and away and drop you just where you want to get down. I once wrote a song about it; it began something like this:

The fairy folk move through the sky
Faster far than eagles fly.
Their fairy steeds so swiftly run
That journeys end when they're begun.

'But you've got to be careful. There was once a man who refused to believe that such a journey was possible; and so he cried out 'Horse and Hattock' just to show, he said, that nothing would happen. But the fairies carried him up and away and dropped him in the king's treasure-house where he was found by the king's guards, and they, in turn, refused to believe him when he tried to explain to them how he came to be where he was found; which, indeed, made him feel quite uncomfortable in more ways than one.'

Amid all these explanations, and all this talking, Borrobil had been looking to right and to left as though expecting someone to join them. And now suddenly he gave a hail, which was at once answered from the valley below. Both the children had been so absorbed in all he had been telling them that they had quite forgotten their own adventure. But at once they knew what that hail meant.

'Morac!' cried Jean. And Morac it was. Soon Morac and Giric had ridden up, leading at loose-rein the children's two shaggy ponies. Then was there much talking and explaining. Giric, the taciturn, stood by, adding only a word now and then; but Borrobil, Morac, and the children had much to say and then more to say again. At length Borrobil spoke of King Brude's command that Sulig should die.

'Die he shall,' said Morac simply. Giric nodded his head. But the children felt awed and frightened at the thought of death for the man who had held them in his power so shortly before. 'What say you, Borrobil?' asked Morac. 'How best shall King Brude be obeyed and our own vengeance fulfilled?'

But Borrobil was not listening. He had stepped to one side and was standing intent, with a distant look in his eyes. All of them watched him.

'Sulig is free,' he said at last. 'The Black Sulig turned himself into a mole and has just succeeded in burrowing his way out. Something like that I expected. And that was why I knew my magic spell could not keep him for ever beneath the earth. But I did not know how deep he was when I bound him there, nor what shape he would take to regain the air. So I could not know how long it would take him to win free again.'

'What do we do now?' asked Morac.

'Wait,' answered Borrobil. 'We must see first what the Black Sulig will do.' Again he looked into the distant places their own eyes could not reach. And as he looked so he described all things as they took place.

'The mole is once more the man. He has entered his castle-gate. He has reached the hall. He takes parchment and writes. He calls the red-headed dwarf and gives him the parchment. The dwarf leaves the hall; now he is passing out of the castle-gate.'

Borrobil stopped. He brought back his eyes to Morac. 'We must get that message,' he said quickly. 'We must learn to whom it goes and what it says.'

CHAPTER II

The Message

BORROBIL, Morac, and Giric had had their heads together for so long that Donald and Jean were sure the dwarf would have delivered his message and would have returned to Sulig's castle long before the three of them had made up their minds what to do. It was awful having to wait like this while those three talked and talked and talked. But their period of waiting was over. The group broke up. Borrobil and Morac, both looking thoroughly satisfied with themselves, came over to join the children, while Giric, without a word, slipped into the wood.

'Well, at any rate that shows how useful it is to know all the paths of every wood and every forest,' said Borrobil complacently.

'Ah! but how can you tell *which* path the dwarf will take?' asked Jean.

'There is only one path the dwarf *can* take now,' answered Borrobil. 'That was why we had to wait so long before Giric could set off to intercept him. All the time have I been watching him carefully, and now there is only one path left to him, and that is the path leading to the giant's cave. It looks as though Sulig is sending his message to the giant Grugol – doubtless a message asking for the giant's help. And when we see what the Black Sulig has said then we shall know what action to take. We must wait, but, you know, waiting may yet be comfortable –

> '*A fool stands up when a wise man sits*
> *While both have legs only one has wits.*'

And suiting his actions to his words, Borrobil sat down facing the depths of the wood. Donald and Jean quickly sat down one on each side of him; and Morac stretched out on the ground full length near by.

For a time the children were silent. Really, too many things had been happening in too short a time. It was nice just to sit and have no more excitements and adventures. Also, every time they turned towards Borrobil he seemed to have that distant look in his eyes which they knew meant that he was watching both Giric and the dwarf inside the depths of the forest. Then a thought struck Donald, and he felt bound to speak. 'But, Borrobil,' he exclaimed, 'if Giric takes the message from the dwarf the giant won't get it, and although we shall know what Sulig wrote to the giant the dwarf is sure to tell Sulig that the message was taken from him and that won't help us very much.'

'True,' answered Borrobil. 'But Giric will bring the message back here; we shall read it; then Giric will give it back to the dwarf and send him on his journey again to deliver it to Grugol. So that settles everything.'

Donald puzzled it over, and still it didn't seem to make sense.

'But the dwarf will *know* you've read it, and he'll tell Grugol and Grugol will tell Sulig and that will spoil it all.'

'True, again,' said Borrobil. 'But *will* the dwarf know that we took the message from him, that we read it, and that we gave it back to him again? Indeed, how much he will know depends partly on his own stupidity, of which we are sure, and partly too on our plan and on Giric's success in carrying it out. No! I'm not going to tell you what the plan is,' he added, as he saw Donald getting ready to ask. 'Wait until Giric comes back *the second time* and both of you shall hear all about it.'

That seemed to be final; and Borrobil's tone had clearly indicated that he wanted to be free to watch what was going on in the forest without too many interruptions.

Obviously there was nothing to do but to wait. Borrobil was most annoying, and he was even more annoying still, when, a little later, they heard him give a low chuckle which meant that he had seen something they couldn't see. Not only was he annoying, he was most unfair. 'Wait for Giric to come back *the second time*,' Donald kept thinking to himself. 'Why the second time?' It was all very puzzling, and he was still wondering what the plan could be and how 'the second time' came into it, when Giric stepped out of the trees. In his hand he held a roll of parchment. Borrobil looked at him, questioningly. Giric smiled and nodded his head. Then he handed the parchment to Borrobil. Borrobil unrolled it and, while they all clustered round him, he read aloud:

'*The Black Sulig to the mighty Grugol,* GREETING. KNOW *that I have grave fears for thy safety and mine. Only by the exercise of all my powers have I but recently escaped from the trickery of him who is called Borrobil. And it is known to me that Morac, the slayer of the dragon, is also within these parts. Unless we move to defend ourselves I see no other end but one; and that one a like end for both of us. Yet by good fortune are Borrobil and Morac much concerned with the safety of two stranger children who accompany them on their way to the north. And their way must be through the pass of the river. If it seem good to thee, then take up thy place behind the tall stone at the head of the pass, and there await their coming. Conceal thyself well. If the man called Giric rides first, let him pass thee by. But watch carefully for Morac. Strike hard as he passes thee. And strike quickly ere he can draw the sword Greysteel which is now his. With the fool Borrobil I will deal myself. That I may be known to thee I shall come to the stone in the form of a white pigeon. The strength of two is greater than the strength of one. Thine own peril binds thee to this encounter. The bearer can be trusted to bring back an answer. An answer therefore give to him that I may know this message has safely reached thee by the right bearer, and that when I come to the stone at the head of the pass so shall I find thee hidden there.*'

Morac's eyes flashed, and his hand fell on the hilt of Greysteel. 'So they would strike me from behind,' he muttered. But Borrobil gave one chuckle after another, and his grin seemed to run from ear to ear and back again. 'A written word is a secret lost,' he said; 'and that's as good a saying as any. The message can now go on its way to Grugol.' He re-rolled the parchment, returned it to Giric, and Giric once more slipped back into the trees.

'So Sulig has tricked Grugol to come to his aid,' he said, half to himself and half to Morac and the children. 'Well, we have long known the giant Grugol as the worst and most cruel robber throughout the length and breadth of the land; but what with the curse of the dragon, and what with one trouble after another, he has had everything his own way far too long. Hitherto no danger has faced him. Until now. But now two birds shall we catch at this same tall stone. And Morac shall try how truly the sword Greysteel can strike.' He stopped; and again the children could see that he was watching Giric and the dwarf in the depths of the wood.

And now the time seemed to pass more slowly than ever. Would Giric never come back 'the second time'? It was all so very puzzling. 'But,' Donald kept thinking and thinking, 'but the dwarf is sure to tell Grugol that the message was taken from him on the way, and then given back to him again, and he is sure to tell Sulig also; and that means that neither Sulig nor Grugol will go to the stone, but they will both do something else just as nasty but quite different. I do wish Borrobil wouldn't be so mysterious about it all.' As for Jean, she had given it up, and was wondering to herself why there were dwarfs and what made them, and why some men were giants and some men dwarfs, when Giric stepped out of the trees 'the second time'. And, quite unlike Giric, he was actually smiling; indeed, almost laughing.

'All over!' he said. 'Grugol has sent back the dwarf bidding him tell Sulig that he will await him at the stone. And Grugol himself has already set forth.'

'Come then,' cried Morac. 'The sword Greysteel shall indeed show how truly it can strike.' And he moved towards the horses tethered to the trees.

'But Borrobil!' cried Donald, 'you said you would tell us all about your plan and everything else as soon as Giric came back "the second time". And now you are going to rush off again without telling us anything at all.'

'And so we were,' confessed Borrobil. 'I forgot. I am truly sorry. And why should there be any haste? Let us wait awhile so that the mighty Grugol may be the stiffer in his joints after crouching long behind the stone. That should make it easier for Morac.' And he grinned mischievously in Morac's direction. The feeling of restraint and worry seemed to have completely vanished. Borrobil was as pleased and merry and excited as ever he had been.

'Come, Giric,' he continued, 'come and tell the children the tale of your adventures with the dwarf.'

But Giric drew back. 'I am no weaver of tales,' he muttered. 'He lives long who keeps his tongue to help with his eating.'

'A true saying,' cried Borrobil, 'but I gave my promise to the children that they should know all when you came back "the second time", and a promise given is like a bird that is set free from a cage – it cannot be recalled.'

'A true saying, also,' agreed Giric, 'and since the promise was given to the children I am willing to tell as good a tale as ever I heard any man tell; and that is the tale of a dwarf, a message and a sore head.'

CHAPTER 12

Giric's Tale

'IT's a good tale,' said Giric slowly, 'and one that's worth the telling.'

As you know, Borrobil had watched the dwarf until it was clear he was making for the giant's cave. Then came my turn – to get ahead of the dwarf and to relieve him of his message. That was when you saw me slip away into the trees of the wood.

To get ahead of the dwarf was easy, for I had the shorter way to go; and already we had agreed upon a plan to relieve him of the message. Much depended upon the dwarf's stupidity of which we had heard and knew. And therein Borrobil was right as in everything else; for soon you will agree that never was a more stupid man sent on another's errand. Nevertheless, to agree upon a plan, and to carry it out, are two quite different things. Yet almost at once I saw the very place for the part I had to play. Indeed, I was standing on it. For, where I stood, the path to the cave ran by the side of a lake. And while the lake was on one side of the path, on the other side were the ruins of a small cattle-fold or hut, one stone wall and part of the roof still remaining. Soon I had climbed to the roof; soon I had loosened one of the biggest stones; and then there I was, lying flat, well-hidden, and all ready to drop my big stone fair and square on the dwarf's head as he passed on his way beneath.

Nor had I long to wait. Along came the dwarf, going surprisingly fast for the shortness of his legs, but not too fast for me to drop the stone bang on the top of his big red poll. Down he went; and then down I came to have a look at him. At the first look I thought I had chosen too big a stone, for he lay very

crumpled and very still; but I was soon reassured. I had only put him to sleep for a while and my first reckoning was correct – that no stone would be too big for that thick red head. And there, lying on the ground beside him, was the message as it had dropped out of his hand when he fell. There it was, just waiting for me to pick it up and to come back here with it, so that Borrobil might know all that the Black Sulig had planned. That was when I came back 'for the first time'.

That done, and Borrobil and all of you knowing everything that Sulig had written to the giant Grugol, back again I went to the dwarf with the parchment message all neatly rolled as before. He was still lying where I had left him. I placed the parchment on the ground by his side, and began to try to wake him up by throwing water over his head. It was not an easy task, for although the lake was just by, there was nothing in which to carry the water save one of the dwarf's own shoes. And a shoe doesn't hold much water to start with, and far less by the time you've carried it even a short distance. Nor did I like the work overmuch, for the more I threw water over the dwarf's face the uglier it seemed to become. But I kept on; and after a time he opened his eyes, gave a grunt, and shut his eyes again. That was encouraging anyway. So I watered him still more. Again he opened his eyes, and this time he sat up.

'Where am I?' he asked; and seeing me standing there with one of his own shoes full of water, and feeling his head and neck all running wet, he reached out for his club.

'Steady, master,' I said. 'Where would you be if I hadn't helped you?' That seemed to make him think. He sat there muttering to himself, feeling his head tenderly, and glowering at me. And a pretty sight he looked. The stone had grazed some of the skin away and the blood was still coming down his face in thin trickles; while as for the shape of his head, it looked as though a large lump had begun to grow out of it.

'Better?' I asked; but he didn't answer. Instead he looked round, and his eye falling on the parchment lying beside him, hastily he picked it up and thrust it inside his coat. Then he got up.

'Shall I help you, master?' I asked.

'No,' he said shortly, and he turned on me. 'You saw me cracked over the head?' he asked.

'Yes,' said I.

'Were you here?' he says suspiciously.

'No, master,' I replied. 'I was not here' (and that was surely true for I was on the roof of the ruined fold).

'But you were near enough to see it all happen?'

'That I was,' said I.

'Oh,' he says, 'then you can tell me who it was.'

'That I can,' said I.

'Come,' he cries, 'who cracked me over the head?'

'Well, if you must know his name, master . . .' I began, when he interrupts me angrily –

'Who was it?'

'Diddit Meself,' I answers.

'Diddit Meself,' says he. 'It's a queer name, but I shall remember it the better.' And with that he turns his back to me and off he goes on his way with never a word of thanks for all I'd done. (And as Giric said that, Donald could have sworn he saw him wink slyly at Borrobil.)

So far all had gone well; but I had yet to be sure that Grugol wouldn't be asking any difficult questions. So I followed the dwarf closely until he reached the cave, and there, by hiding behind a thick bush, I was able to hear and see all that passed.

Up came the dwarf; and there, sitting at his ease in front of his cave, was the giant Grugol.

'Greetings from Sulig to the brave Grugol,' says the dwarf.

'Greetings to thee,' answers Grugol.

'My master sends this message,' says the dwarf, handing over the parchment. Grugol takes it and reads it; he frowns; he nods; and finally he goes into the cave, coming out again with his big two-handed sword.

'So Morac and Borrobil would like to play with me,' he says grimly, looking hard at the dwarf. And as he looks, so for the first time he notices the dwarf's head.

'That was a mighty crack,' he says.

'Yes,' answers the dwarf shortly.

'And you gave a harder crack in return?' he asks.

'No,' answers the dwarf shortly.

'What!' roars Grugol. 'Only one cracked head instead of two? Who cracked your head like that and still went scatheless? Perhaps it was the dragon-slaying Morac?'

'No,' says the dwarf shortly.

'Yes; No; No,' roars the giant. 'Fine talk that! Are all your answers in one word? I'm asking you: who cracked your head?'

'Diddit Meself,' says the dwarf shortly.

'Oh,' says Grugol, calming down. 'Now I see. No wonder you're not anxious to talk. Well, I'm not anxious to hear more of it. Tell your master I shall await him behind the tall stone at the head of the pass. And as for yourself, go to the back of my cave where you'll find a pot of healing salve. That should level that lump a little. "Diddit Meself," says you, truculently. Well, I hope your head runs into something softer next time.' And away goes Grugol to hide behind the stone at the head of the pass.

The dwarf wanders into the cave. And when he comes out shortly afterwards I think to myself that I wouldn't mind some of that healing salve either. For scarcely could I see a sign of the crack I had given him, and the lump had completely disappeared. There was no doubt that when he got back with Grugol's answer the Black Sulig would notice nothing amiss. But I had still to wait till he'd gone. And as he passed me, I, still hiding myself behind the bush, could hear him muttering away 'Diddit Meself! That fellow shall pay for this crack. One cracked head instead of two! That there shall be next time also. And with a name like Diddit Meself he should be easy to find.'

'And so I came back "for the second time",' ended Giric;

and the tale is as good a tale as any I know. While better still, Sulig and Grugol have played into our hands.'

'And you said you were no weaver of tales!' cried Borrobil. 'But now Morac is as impatient to be off as any old war-horse. He is anxious to see how Greysteel will bite into the giant Grugol. And Sulig is waiting for "the old fool Borrobil". It would be a pity to keep him waiting too long.'

CHAPTER 13

How Grugol was Slain, and How Sulig Met his Fate

AGAIN the children were mounted on their shaggy ponies. But this time the order of their going was different. First went Giric as before; then, but far behind him, came Morac; then, and again far behind, came Donald and Jean with Borrobil walking close at their horses' heads. Donald had said that he would walk and that Borrobil could have his pony; then he had said that he and Jean would ride on the one pony so that Borrobil could have the other. But Borrobil insisted on walking. He said he preferred it; he said it would do him good; and finally he said that if Donald didn't ride on and stop pestering him he would be really angry.

Again, too, they were continuing their way up the narrow mountain pass, though now, behind the high, wooded hills that rose steeply on either side, occasional glimpses could be caught of far-away mountains capped with snow. The pass was narrow; so narrow that there were only two ways to go – to go on, or to go back. Both the children were somewhat frightened and very subdued. Were they always to be shut in like this on every journey? Was every journey to be like that first journey of all, the journey to the wood? And now they were riding on, knowing full well that somewhere – at the head of the pass – they would come to a tall stone behind which a giant would be lurking, and on the top of which a black magician would be perched in the shape of a white pigeon. Perhaps, in their hearts, both of them wished that they were riding the other way, going back to the safety of King Brude's castle. True, Borrobil, Morac, and Giric were with them; but it was something more than that – pride possibly, or courage, or perhaps both pride and courage – that made them try to look unconcerned and wholly unconscious of the danger ahead.

And then, in the distance, dim and shadowy, stood a tall grey stone – the stone at the head of the pass! Donald turned to look

at Borrobil. Borrobil smiled cheerfully back at him. That made him feel brave again, and although his heart was pounding he felt certain that all would be well. Jean, too, turned to Borrobil, and to her he said, 'Trust to Morac'.

'Of course I do,' answered Jean stoutly; and she meant it.

Nearer and nearer they drew to that fateful stone. Now Donald thought he could see a white speck on the top of the stone. 'That will be Sulig,' he said to himself. Then he lost it again, and thought that he must have imagined it. Nearer and nearer they drew. Now Giric was almost level with the stone! He had reached it! He had passed it! Nothing had happened. Now Morac in turn was drawing closer to the stone! Donald's heart seemed to be pounding harder than ever. Something was bound to happen soon. And something did.

Giric was well past the stone, and Morac had not quite reached it, when Giric suddenly turned, and with a shout began to gallop quickly back towards Morac. Morac stopped. Giric gave another shout, and raised his hand high above his head.

And what of the giant Grugol as he crouched behind the stone? As Giric raised his shout and began to gallop quickly back towards Morac, so doubt and confusion seized the giant's mind. Was his hiding-place discovered? Was Giric riding back to warn Morac? That signal could have no other meaning. Yet if that were so, surely it would be better to strike at Morac forthwith, swiftly, suddenly, before Giric's warning could be understood, and while Morac was still unaware of the danger that lurked ahead? Were he to let Giric come too close he might then lose all chance of one fatal unsuspected blow. More than that, he might himself be trapped between Morac and Giric, with two foes to fight instead of one. So ran the giant Grugol's thought. And Grugol made up his mind. Out he stepped from behind the stone, holding high his big two-handed sword above his head. Out he stepped, and there, some twenty paces away from him, stood Morac, dismounted and the magic Greysteel in his hand.

Grugol paused; but not for long. In two massive strides he covered the twenty paces that lay between. Down came his sword in one mighty blow. Yet as he struck, so Morac lightly stepped aside. The sword sang in the air as it swept past him; a shudder ran up its length as it bit the earth. But even as its

edge cut deep into the ground, so came Morac's answer. High in the air shone the magic blade; it flashed and fell; and as it fell so its note rang out clear and true like a note plucked from a noble harp. And scarce had Greysteel met the giant's helm than in turn it cut into the ground between the giant's feet. Yet no shudder ran through Morac's sword as it bit the earth.

Grugol looked hard at Morac. 'Is that all your magic sword can do?' he asked, and there was scorn within his voice. 'It touches me but as a feather. I feel it but as a trickle of water that runs down my back. As I thought, its magic has perished with long years in the yew. Now shall I show you how deeper my own two-handed sword can cut.'

But Morac stood fast. Nor did he lift Greysteel to his aid.

'Strike, Grugol,' was all he said.

Grugol's eyes flashed. Was this to be his turn? Would Morac indeed stand thus, awaiting his blow, the sword Greysteel idle by his side? He began to lift once more his massive brand; but, as the sword-tip hovered on the ground, so a new look crept into his eyes, a look of astonishment, followed swiftly by a look of fear. The sword dropped out of helpless hands, and the giant frame, cut neatly in two by the magic Greysteel, divided and fell apart, crashing to the ground on either side of Morac.

'That was indeed a noble cut,' said Morac softly to himself as he stepped away, 'a cut from helm to toe, and he felt it but as a trickle of water down his back.' And with that Morac slid his blade back into its scabbard where, as it ran cleanly home, it sang with a low purring sound as though well content with all its work.

And what of Sulig? Even as Sulig in his message to the giant had promised to take care 'of the fool Borrobil' while Grugol struck treacherously at Morac from behind the stone, so had Borrobil agreed to 'take care' of Sulig while Morac fought the giant. Nor did Borrobil fail to play his part.

Almost at the very moment when Giric turned and raised his shout, Donald and Jean heard Borrobil make his call. It was one word only, but it sounded like a summons that must be obeyed. And as Borrobil made that call, so from the sky above they saw a falcon falling like a plummet upon the white pigeon that perched on the tall grey stone. Yet just in time the Black Sulig saw his peril. As the falcon clutched with its talons, so he turned himself into an adder and slithering within a crack that ran down the stone made his way quickly to the ground. Once there, the adder that was Sulig began to crawl to the shelter of the thick gorse that grew around. What then the Black Sulig would have done cannot be known. For fate overtook the evil magician on his last journey. Nearly had he reached the gorse that would have yielded shelter and concealment too, when Morac, stepping aside from the slain Grugol, brought down his heel upon the adder's head. It cracked like an egg. A shiver ran through the loathsome thing; it writhed once, twice; it lay still. The Black Sulig was dead.

Borrobil came slowly up. 'And so you have slain both the mighty Grugol and the evil Sulig. It was well done.'

Morac turned, astonished. 'How so?' he asked. 'The good Greysteel has served me well, and there lies one who will not be mourned,' he said, pointing to the dead giant. 'But the Black Sulig I left to you.'

'True,' said Borrobil. 'But there lies the Black Sulig.' In turn he pointed, and he pointed to the adder that lay crushed by Morac's heel.

Morac looked. He passed his hand over his eyes. 'The dragon's skin,' he said in a hushed voice. 'I remember now. When first the children were carried away I saw Sulig lying crushed and broken like an adder trodden under a man's heel.'

There was silence for a moment. And in that silence they heard from the forest far away the faint echo of some mighty crash.

'So has his castle fallen,' said Borrobil. 'So have the pillars of sand been broken. The evil man and his evil work have perished together. It is right that it should be so.'

'And so may all that is evil perish,' added Morac simply.

But the children stood by, silent, frightened. Perhaps now they could go safely on their way to bring back the Princess Finella? Or were they to face other dangers, other perils yet?

CHAPTER 14

The Story of Glastil

'COME,' said Borrobil, 'we must be on our way. Morac will appear laggard in love if he takes too long to reach Finella'; and he grinned merrily at all of them.

'But how can you come with us', asked Donald, 'when you haven't a horse, and when you won't take mine and let me share with Jean?'

'True,' answered Borrobil, and a mischievous look came into his eyes. 'True. I need a horse. A horse I need. Where shall I get a horse? Oh, where can a horse be found? A horse! A horse! A horse I need.'

'Stop it!' cried Jean, 'and don't be silly.'

But Borrobil paid no attention. 'A horse! A horse! A horse I want. A horse I need.'

'Oh, do stop it, and be sensible,' cried both the children together.

'But,' protested Borrobil, 'if I keep on calling like this for long enough, I'm sure to get *a little hoarse*. And a little horse is all I need.'

Donald and Jean just looked at him.

'All right. I'm sorry,' said Borrobil, looking so ridiculously contrite that everyone had to laugh. 'But all the same I still want a horse

> *With twice as many legs as me*
> *And its tail in the place where its head should be.*'

Donald was just about to say 'I do wish you'd be sensible', when it struck him that there was something strange in the last line. He repeated it to himself, and then he looked at Borrobil, only to see that Borrobil was looking at him exactly

as though he wanted him to say, 'Whatever do you mean?'
So he said it: 'Whatever do you mean?'

'Ah, that's a story,' answered Borrobil.

'A story!' cried Jean. 'I do wish you'd tell it us.'

'Just what I want to do. Ever since Giric became our best
story-teller with his tale of the dwarf and the message, I've
been wondering how I could manage to regain my lost reputa-
tion. It's only a short story, very short, and it's a very old one,
but it's a very good one.'

Borrobil, of course, was simply trying to make the children
forget all that they had just seen. And Morac and Giric guessed
as much. They fell in with his mood.

'An old story is like an old friend,' said Morac gravely, 'both
have stood the test of time.'

'And a good story is like good news,' added Giric, 'it cannot
be heard too often.'

Borrobil looked round. 'Agreed?' he asked. 'Right! Well,
this is the story of the horse with its tail where its head should
be.'

Once upon a time in a country far distant from this land there
lived a king called Ostla who was known far and wide for his
many horses. So many horses had King Ostla that he himself
rode a different horse every day in the year, while the captains
in his army had each a different horse for every week. That is
not to say that the king, and each captain, too, had not a
favourite horse that he rode far oftener than all his other horses.
But of the number of horses that the king had, and that each
captain had, there could be no doubt. Three hundred and
sixty-five were the horses of the king, and fifty-two were the
horses of each captain in the king's army. Moreover, all the
king's castles were surrounded by stables; every stable had one
hundred stalls, and always in every stall of every stable there
stood a noble and spirited horse. So great, indeed, was this
king's passion for horses that the highest officer in each of his
castles was the Constable, who was the head of all the stables,
all the stalls, all the horses, and all the many grooms who were

needed to attend to them. Naturally, because of this, the men of King Ostla's land knew far more about horses than did the men of all other lands; and because of this, the great men of the surrounding kingdoms sought to have their horses reared and groomed by men who had served in King Ostla's stables.

Now in one of these neighbouring kingdoms there had lately arrived at the king's castle a groom, Glastil by name, who having left the stable of King Ostla, where he had served faithfully for nine full years, had acquired a deep knowledge of horses and all their ways. This knowledge and his services he had offered to the neighbouring king for a high reward – a reward which the king was glad to pay to secure so excellent a groom. Nor was the king dissatisfied. Under Glastil the king's horses soon became distinguished for their beauty and their strength; and so excellent was the work of Glastil that all paid tribute to the services he had rendered in the king's stables. With all this, moreover, Glastil was a merry man; he would jest often, and so was he the more welcomed, for all men love a good jest. And in his jesting, never was it easy to tell whether he spoke his words in earnest or not, and many a laugh rang through stable and hall because of some merry prank played by the groom Glastil.

Yet often while all others laughed, one man would frown and be silent, and that man was the king's High Steward. No jest of Glastil's pleased him, for he was proud and vain, and to pride and vanity were added jealousy and hatred – jealousy of Glastil's great knowledge of horses, and hatred of Glastil because of the way all men made him welcome. Gladly would the High Steward have sent Glastil back to his own country; but the king was of another mind, deeming that a good groom found should be a good groom kept. So Glastil remained in the king's service and so also hatred of the groom remained in the heart of the king's High Steward.

Now one morning, when Glastil had entered the king's stable to see that all was well with the horses therein, immediately he came running forth again with a look of amazement on his face, crying out that surely the king's horses had

been bewitched overnight. Then, turning round he fastened
the stable door securely behind him, and with that seemed
more content. All who had heard and seen, now came running
up, some asking what evil had befallen the horses of the king,
others asking what should they do. Yet for some time Glastil
would make no reply. At length he confessed that he had that
morning seen the strangest sight of all; for although he had
spent many years tending the horses of kings and great men,
never before had he seen a horse with its tail where its head
should be.

'What!' they all cried at once. 'A horse with its tail where
its head should be! Such a wonder must be seen! Come, Glastil,
open the door and let us in!'

Yet always Glastil refused; and still they urged him to let
them in. And no man noticed the king's High Steward who
had approached and who stood to one side listening to all that
was said.

At last the High Steward stepped forward.

'Open the door, Glastil,' he commanded. 'I order you to
show me this horse so that I may carry the strange tidings to
the king.'

Glastil could not do other than obey. He opened the door.
Together Glastil and the High Steward entered the stable,
being followed therein by a vast crowd, for the news of the
strange wonder had now reached all within the castle-walls.

'Which is the stall?' cried the High Steward. 'Show me the
horse.'

Without speaking, Glastil led him to the furthest end of the
stable, and there, pointing to one of the horses, said but the
one word, 'See'. The High Steward looked, and all those who
had pressed in behind him likewise looked. And at once loud
and great were the laughs that burst forth from all those who
stood beside and behind the king's High Steward. For Glastil
pointed to a horse that he had tethered to the ring of the stall,
not by its head-rope, but by its tail, so that the long tail of the
horse hung down in the corn of the manger 'in the place where
its head should be'.

Filled with rage at the jest thus played upon him in the presence of so many men, the High Steward ordered Glastil to be seized and tied securely within a sack, thereafter ordering the sack with Glastil therein to be hung on the outer side of the castle-gate. So did the High Steward hope that all who passed that way would mock at the groom's unhappy plight, and so did the High Steward hope that thereby he would gain a sweet revenge. And all was done as the king's High Steward ordered. Glastil was seized and hung in the sack on the outer side of the castle-gate.

But not long had Glastil been hanging there than he heard a voice exclaiming 'What's this? A sack hanging from the gate of the king's castle? Never have I seen that before.'

Nor was Glastil slow to perceive that this must be some passing stranger who knew naught of all that had gone before. And perceiving that, forthwith in a loud voice he began to cry out 'O marvellous! O strangely beautiful! How well have I been rewarded for my service to the king! What lovely visions come before mine eyes!'

'Ho! There!' called the stranger. 'Is that a man within the sack? What sights are these you see?'

'Did someone call?' asked Glastil.

'Yes,' replied the stranger. 'Here is one who would like to know many things, and most of all why you are within that sack, whoever you are, and what are the sights you see?'

'Interrupt me not,' answered Glastil, 'but go your way. Such sights as these I shall never see again.

'But first satisfy my curiosity and then I go,' replied the stranger. 'For I am but a traveller passing this way, and although I have travelled far, yet never before have I known of a man, tied in a sack, hanging from the gate of a king's castle, and there seeing strange and marvellous sights.'

'Not a *sack*,' said Glastil, 'but a magic coat turned into the shape of a sack. Know, O stranger, that those whom the king wishes to reward, to them does he grant the honour of being allowed to spend one day tied up in this magic coat hanging on this part of his castle-gate. For once within the coat, and the coat securely tied that the light of day may not enter therein, so forthwith do marvellous visions appear. Already have I seen the vision of the golden chariot drawn by the seven silver steeds and driven by the milk-white maid of wondrous beauty; and when your voice broke in upon me, I had but then feasted my eyes upon the vision of the castle that is built of ivory and rubies and that is guarded by the three black unicorns with hoofs of pearl and horns of chalcedony. That was a truly wondrous sight. What next shall come, I know not. But go! For you spoil this feast which is a feast of but one day.'

'Ah! how I envy you,' exclaimed the stranger, with longing in his voice. 'Would that I were within that magic coat!'

'But you have rendered no service to the king,' replied Glastil. 'Go, I tell you, so that once more I may enjoy these delights of magic scenes.'

'Yet I would gladly pay much gold even to be but a short time within the coat!' cried the stranger.

'No, that cannot be; not even for much gold.'

'But think,' called back the stranger eagerly. 'I would pay you much gold to be within the coat but a short time and then you could yourself return. And when you did return so would the gold be yours as well as all the visions still to come.'

'That is certainly true,' replied Glastil; and he spoke slowly as though weighing in his mind all that the stranger had said. 'Yet, were I to yield to your desire, so would you have to give me your bounden word that you would let me return within the coat immediately one vision had been yours.'

'Granted! Granted!' cried the stranger. 'I give my word. One vision only, and I will let you back again within the coat.'

'And that shall be fifty pieces of gold, no more, no less,' answered Glastil.

'It shall be so! Quick! I give my word and I give the gold.'

'Take down the cost then,' said Glastil, and his voice was the voice of a man who regrets the bargain he has struck. 'But handle it carefully, for I am a man of some weight. Then untie the rope. So, when I have your gold within my purse and your hand upon your word, so shall I let you into the coat, so shall

I tie it securely that the light of day may not enter, so shall I hang you on the gate. But one vision only! One vision and no more.'

'Quickly the stranger took down the sack, untied its neck, and so let Glastil out. Then handing over a purse of gold to the groom, the stranger stepped gladly within the sack himself, urging Glastil to make all haste to tie him securely therein and so to hang him on the castle-gate. All of which Glastil no less quickly and no less gladly did. And having secured the stranger safely within the sack and the stranger's gold safely within his bosom, the merry Glastil made what haste he could to put a long distance between himself and the castle-gate, thinking as he went that for once he had been well paid for a good jest.

'And that is the story of the horse with its tail where its head should be,' ended Borrobil. 'But I have still to find a horse; and yet I know where I can borrow one if you would like to come with me to a fairy knoll.' And Borrobil looked quizzically at Donald and Jean.

'Fairy knoll!' cried both the children at once, forgetting all the questions they had intended to ask about Glastil, the Stranger, the Sack, and whether ostlers were so called because they were all originally grooms of King Ostla. 'Fairy knoll! But we'd love to come.'

'Yes,' answered Borrobil, 'but if you do come, you will have to do everything exactly as I tell you, otherwise the fairies will not lend me a horse, and more than that, we may be kept in their kingdom and find it impossible to leave. But I know of a fairy knoll not far from here; and there we could try to borrow a horse with its head and its tail both in the right places. If we go there, will you promise faithfully and truly to do everything I tell you to do?'

'We will!' they cried. 'We will.'

'Good! We will go. But remember carefully all that I tell you to do; and remember equally carefully all that I tell you not to do. And if you can remember and obey, so will the fairies lend me a horse.'

CHAPTER 15

Inside the Fairies' Knoll

BORROBIL turned to Morac. 'For a while our ways must part. I shall take the children to the Fairy Queen; but your own journey is pressing, and Finella awaits you. It would be better if you and Giric were to ride on. Later we shall come together again at the castle of the Men of Orc. Till then, may all go well with you.'

Morac nodded. 'And with you, too,' he answered. And with that he raised his hand in salute to the children. Giric in turn raised his hand. And the two of them turned their horses' heads to the north, and so rode on.

Donald and Jean had not thought that their visit to the Fairies' Knoll would mean parting from Morac and Giric. Reluctantly they called out 'Good-bye, Good-bye,' and then stood watching them as they made their way up the now widening pass. They grew smaller and smaller in the distance; the way they had covered grew longer and longer; now they could just be seen – two horsemen riding together far away. And Borrobil said, 'Come.'

Leading the children's two ponies by walking between their heads, Borrobil began to climb the steep side of the pass. The way lay through thickets of gorse and shrub; but the way was also short. Soon they had reached a smooth stretch of turf ('Almost like a cricket-field on the side of a hill,' thought Donald to himself) and there, at one end of the smooth stretch, was a grassy knoll. Straight to the knoll walked Borrobil. He loosed the ponies and they moved off to browse on the grass. Then, standing with his back to the knoll, he held out wide his arms as though warning the children to come no farther.

'Here is one entrance to the Fairy Kingdom,' he said. 'Twice shall I knock on the knoll; and by knocking twice in the right place with the right spell, so will a door appear. And when the door appears it will immediately open; for the double knock is the 'knock of good'. That was always so and still is so.' (And here Jean thought at once of the postman's welcome double knock.) 'Always knock twice when visiting the fairies or friends. To knock once will bring no answer. With one knock come bad tidings and unwelcome guests. No one answers the single knock. So I shall knock twice. And as the door appears and opens, so forthwith shall I thrust my knife in the lintel, so that the door may not be shut again without first removing the knife. By so doing the anger of the Fairy Queen will descend upon me; but I must hope to be forgiven. For only by so doing can the door be kept open to await our return. And that is because the fairies will neither touch nor pass any iron fashioned by man. Then we shall pass in.

'Once we are inside, remember these my two warnings, and never forget them. And the two warnings are – in the first place, accept no present save one. Whatever delightful or precious thing may be offered to you, refuse to accept it, saying you could not think of taking it, but that gladly would you accept the Moonstone if that were to be offered to you. Always, if any gift is proferred, refuse it, but ask for the Moonstone. And when that is given, take it. We shall need it. And when our need is over, the Moonstone will return to the Fairy Queen. But should you take any other gift, the gift you take will bind you to the fairies for evermore; in taking any other gift so will you take away all chance of your return to earth.

'And in the second place, touch no running water. To touch with hand or foot the water running through their land is to fetter your hands and feet to the fairies' kingdom, so that never again can you return to the land of men.

'These are my warnings. If you remember them, all will be well. A horse will be provided for me by the fairies, and you will have one brief view of the fairy kingdom – something you can never hope to see again. If anything should befall, then watch me and do as I do. The fairies are the kindest of people;

but they love children, and they will want to keep you for ever. And now, after all this, do you still want to come?'

'Yes,' they said, almost in a whisper; for although it was all most exciting, Borrobil had said everything in such a serious way that it was also all rather frightening.

'Right, then. Remember! No present save one, the Moonstone; and touch no running water.' And Borrobil leant forward and knocked on the grassy knoll, once; twice.

Almost as soon as he had lifted his hand from the second knock, the children were startled to see a doorway appear, and almost as soon as it appeared, the door swung slowly inwards. Quickly Borrobil whipped out his knife and thrust it deep into the lintel of the doorway, so that now it was impossible to shut the door without first removing the knife. Then, beckoning the children to follow, he passed through the door and into the knoll.

Donald and Jean had expected to find everything in darkness, and here came their first surprise. For within the door they found themselves in a pale blue light that seemed to be reflected from the roof; but when they looked up to the roof, it seemed to be high above them as if it were part of the blue sky of summer. The grassy knoll had been only a small hillock, but now they were in an immense space, surrounded by a pale blue light, and walking towards a brighter light ahead, just as though the grey light of dawn had become pale blue and they were walking towards the rising sun. Soon they had neared the brighter light ahead, and both of them were wondering what they would see then, when suddenly they found themselves before two crystal doors. The doors swung wide open at their approach, and as they passed through they entered the brightness of the fairy kingdom.

The children gave a cry of delight. Before them they saw a green hill fringed with trees, and with fresh running streams cascading down to a lake that shone like silver in the valley below. The air seemed to be filled with soft music. Everywhere there were fairies. All were dressed in green, and all seemed to be busy. At the entrance to a cave in the side of the hill were fairy smiths hammering out a sword on an anvil; by the side of the lake a number of fairies were spinning a fine gossamer silk, while near by others were weaving the fine silk into a long strip, its sheen as radiant as a rainbow.

'Oh, but it's lovely!' cried Jean.

'It's the very best thing I've ever seen,' Donald admitted slowly. 'I expect that's a magic sword they're making in that cave. One like Morac's. And when they've finished the blade they'll put runes upon it, and they'll put precious stones in the hilt. I wish I had a sword like that.'

'But we will give you one,' said a voice at his side. Donald looked down. And there was a fairy! Certainly there had been no fairy there a moment before. 'Come with me,' said the fairy, 'and you shall try the finest sword we've made in the last ten thousand years. If you like it, it shall be yours. A sword fit for a hero.'

Donald was about to say how marvellous that would be when, just in time, he remembered the first of Borrobil's warnings.

'No, thank you,' he said politely. 'It's very nice of you, but I couldn't think of accepting it. But if you'd like to give me the Moonstone . . .' And as he said the word 'Moonstone' the fairy was gone.

'What a near escape,' he thought to himself, and he began walking towards the weavers by the lake. Ahead of him he could see that Jean had already reached the lake and was talking to the fairies spinning and weaving there. For a brief moment he wondered how she could have got there so quickly, but almost as the thought passed through his mind, and certainly before he had taken more than a few steps, he found that he also had reached the lake! That was queer! Perhaps all walking was like that in the fairy kingdom! Possibly in the fairy kingdom everyone got about as quickly as Borrobil when he travelled on Hattock's Horse. Then he heard Jean talking to the fairies and asking if she could try to weave, too.

'Of course you can,' they said. 'But first you must wash your hands, so that the fine silk may show not the slightest soil. Run over there, and wash you hands in the stream. Then we will show you how to weave sunlight and moonlight into radiant silk.'

Jean was so accustomed to being told to wash her hands before she did this or before she touched that, that away she ran to the stream without a second thought. She knelt down by the bank and had almost dipped her hands in the sparkling water, when something seemed to run in her mind like a line of poetry she had learned at school. 'Dip your hands in running water.' Was that it? No! Suddenly she remembered Borrobil's warning – 'Touch no running water!'

She jumped back from the stream. A look of fear in her eyes gradually gave way to a look of disappointment. She glanced down at her hands. 'But they aren't very dirty anyway,' she thought, 'and perhaps I needn't wash them after all.' Back, hopefully, she went to the fairy group. 'Please can't I still try to weave,' she said. 'My hands aren't really dirty, but I can't wash them for Borrobil said I wasn't to touch any running water.'

At once a look of dismay spread through the group. The fairies stepped back from her, and gathering up their tiny looms ran hastily away across the green meadows. All hope of Jean's weaving had gone. 'Oh, I don't love Borrobil any more,' she cried, stamping her foot. 'I hate him. All the fairies have run away just when I could have woven my lovely silk! Why shouldn't we take any present? Why shouldn't we touch running water? I like presents. I like water. I like dipping my hands in a stream. I like silk. And I don't see why Borrobil should stop us. I don't love him at all. And anyway, what would happen if I did wash my hands and then learned how to weave silk of sunlight and moonlight together?' And she turned away so that Donald wouldn't see the tears that were ready to come.

> 'Who the warnings disobeys
> In the fairy kingdom stays
> Seven years and seven days.'

There stood Borrobil! 'That's the answer,' he said. 'And one day in the fairy kingdom is one hundred years in the land of men.'

Jean slowly lifted her face to look at him. There was a short silence. 'A hundred years a day,' she whispered to herself. 'Seven years and seven days!' The thought was terrifying. 'Oh, Borrobil!' she said in a low voice, 'Oh, I am glad I didn't dip my hands in the running stream.' A further silence; then, 'I'm sorry I was cross, Borrobil.'

'And I'm jolly glad I didn't take that sword they offered to me,' added Donald. 'But my fairy disappeared as soon as I mentioned the Moonstone, and all Jean's fairies ran away when she told them she couldn't wash her hands in the stream. Why was that?'

'Ah,' answered Borrobil gravely, 'Jean's group of fairies ran away because they were ashamed of themselves. They knew that they had tried to trick her into washing her hands in the stream; and when Jean came back and told them she had been warned to touch no running water they thought she must know they had tried to keep her with them by means of an unfair trick. And so they ran away, just like both of you turn your faces away when you have done something of which you are ashamed. But you mustn't blame them. They are really the kindest of people, but they simply love children, and they wanted so much to keep you with them. But also, because they are kind, they can never say "No" when asked for something or when asked to do something. And that was why your fairy disappeared, Donald. Your fairy could not give you the Moonstone, for the Moonstone can be granted only by the Fairy Queen. And so, rather than say "No", your fairy faded away. But when we meet the Fairy Queen you will find that she will hand the Moonstone to one of you, and we shall need it; and to me, if I can pass the test, she will grant the loan of a horse.'

Even as he spoke, there was the Fairy Queen, standing in front of them! Like all the other fairies she was dressed in green, but somehow, in some way, she seemed different from all the others. Jean knew she was the Fairy Queen because of her lovely crown that seemed to be set with stars; and Donald found himself again making the best bow he could, just as he had done when he stood before King Brude.

'The children have learned well,' said the Fairy Queen. 'They are wise and good. They obey in all things, yet hesitate

not to ask why there are some things they are told to do, and some things they are told not to do. The Moonstone I freely grant to serve their need. Yet even more than that do I give to them. The Moonstone shall serve their present need; but, for the future, in a time of great danger that shall come upon them, I make them a gift of the white sea-spray. As the Moonstone shall serve them now, so shall the white sea-spray serve them in their time of greatest need. These are my gifts to the children. As for you, whom men call Borrobil, the purpose of your visit is known. Yet first must you pass the test.'

'I offer myself willingly,' answered Borrobil.

'Then the questions shall be put,' said the Fairy Queen, 'and the first question is this:

> *With water is a basket filled;*
> *No drop of water lost or spilled.*

'Oh dear,' thought Donald to himself, 'riddles. Whatever can the answer to that one be? A sponge? No. That isn't a basket. Perhaps it's a basket under the sea. That would do.'

But Borrobil gave him no time to puzzle further –

> '*With snow I pack my basket tight*
> *And safely carry water white,*'

came his reply.

'The answer is right,' said the Fairy Queen. 'And the second question is this:

> *Now high, now low, now up, now down;*
> *No king ere wore a brighter crown.*'

Jean at once pictured in her mind the bright brass pendulum of the big clock in the house where they were staying for their holidays. 'Now up, now down.' But no king could wear *that* for a crown.

Yet again Borrobil seemed to have no difficulty. Almost without pausing he replied:

> '*The sun will rise, the sun will set;*
> *No crown has reached its splendour yet.*'

'The answer is right for the second time,' said the Fairy
Queen. 'Now for the third question:

> *I'm heard, I'm felt, I'm never seen;*
> *I'm here, I'm gone. Who knows I've been?'*

Harder and harder, thought Donald. But Borrobil didn't
seem to think so. He replied on the instant:

> ' *I hear and feel the winds that blow.*
> *What man their wayward path can know?'*

'The answer is right for the third time,' said the Fairy,
Queen. 'Your wish is granted. A horse has been found for you;
and is even now tethered to the third tree on the right of the
knoll. He will bear you safely. When your need of him is over
turn the horse loose. My people will take care of him and
return him to the place whence he was borrowed. Your
knowledge of all our ways is great; though I like not those who
hold open the portals of my kingdom with cold iron. But your
services on earth are honourable, and my people take joy in
service. May your power for good be still great.'

Borrobil bowed low to the ground, but said not a word.

Next the Fairy Queen bade Donald come to her and hold
out his hand. He advanced shyly, and in his open palm the
queen placed the Moonstone, its rays sparkling white, sometimes pure white, sometimes white tinged with blue.

'The Moonstone is yours to meet your need,' she said. 'No
human being can enter my kingdom and leave my kingdom by
the same path. The door in the knoll is still open, but you must
find your way to the door by another and a darker path. Yet
on that darker path keep the Moonstone always before you. So
long as the fire burns bright and white within its heart, so are
you on the right way. But if the fire within its heart should
pale and die, then halt, move not forward until you are sure
your steps are right. Be guided in your way by the Moonstone's
fire. Yet this my one command you must observe – once you
have passed the portals of my kingdom and have returned

again to human ken, then quickly must you throw the stone away from you lest it bring evil instead of good. It is meant to serve you only for a little while. When its service has been rendered, cast it aside, and it will return to my keeping.'

Donald listened intently to every word. He looked at the Moonstone within his hand, and blushing deeply said in a whisper, 'Thank you, your Majesty.'

The queen bent her head graciously, and turned to Jean. 'And to you I make my gift of the white sea-spray. You shall see the spray for only a little while, even as the Moonstone can be held only for a little while. But the white spray of the salt sea water shall render great aid even when your need is great.'

Jean, open-eyed, could only say 'Thank you'. She said it sincerely, even though she did feel a little disappointed that she was not to see or to hold the white sea-spray at once, but would have to wait for it, to have it or to see it some time later, she didn't know when, or where, or how.

And now the Fairy Queen made a sign, and a fairy smith stood in attendance. She made another sign, and with his hammer he struck the ground before them. At once the ground opened, showing a path leading downwards. Borrobil, still keeping silent, began to descend the path; and Donald and Jean, not knowing what else to do, followed him. Down they went; down; down. And then, suddenly, all was pitch dark. The ground had closed in above them.

'Oh,' cried Jean, and clutched out to reach Borrobil. But she couldn't find him. 'Borrobil! Borrobil!' she cried. Then she heard Donald calling out: 'It's burning with a white light! See! It's all right! The heart of the Moonstone is burning white. We are on the right path.'

'But I can't find you,' cried Jean.

Then Borrobil broke in. 'Don't be afraid, Jean,' he called cheerfully. 'If Donald will hold out his hand at arm's length, so will you see the glow of the Moonstone within it. Then walk towards the glow and you will join him. Thus we shall be together again. Then, if Donald walks slowly forward with the Moonstone before him, we can keep by his side and together we can keep the path. Stand still, Donald, hold out the Moonstone, and we will join you.'

Soon they were all together again; and so began their strange journey in the inky blackness, their only guide the white fire burning in the heart of the Moonstone. The fire burned bright, and they moved steadily on. Then, perhaps because they were going too quickly, or perhaps because they were over-confident, the light suddenly flickered and had gone.

'It's gone,' said Donald, and there was a catch in his voice. But almost at once he remembered that the Moonstone had been given to *him* and that he must show he was worthy of his trust. Somehow that seemed to restore his confidence, and he said, 'I suppose I ought to "cast-about" like bloodhounds do when they've lost the scent. But how do you "cast-about", Borrobil?'

'That should be easy,' answered Borrobil. 'First we will all stand still. Then you shall walk three paces to the right. If nothing happens, turn right-about and walk three paces back to us again. Then shall we know that our way is to the left.'

'But how shall we know?' ask Jean.

'That is simple, Jean,' he replied. 'The fire has already died out in the Moonstone's heart so we know that the way can be neither straight forward nor straight back; it must be to the right or to the left. If Donald tries first the right, and nothing happens, then our way must be towards the left.'

Borrobil and Jean stood close together. Donald, standing by them, turned to the right and walked slowly three paces in that direction. Nothing happened. Turning round, he walked three paces back again, and called to them. They answered just beside him. He put out his hand and it touched Jean's arm. Then, turning to the left, he began to take another three steps. At once the light flickered faintly in the Moonstone's heart.

'It's coming back,' he cried.

'Stop, then,' said Borrobil, 'and we will join you again.' And with Jean he stepped to Donald's side. 'Now must we be more careful. If we move slowly on, so shall we be able to see whether the light grows stronger again, or again begins to die.

And so, by moving slowly to left or to right, gradually we can bring back the full bright light of the fire within the Moon-stone's heart, and thereby know that we are once again on our right path. But always must we walk slowly so that, immediately the fire begins to pale in the very least, we may turn this way or that until it burns brightly once more.'

'Just like a wireless beam for aeroplanes coming in to land,' thought Donald to himself. 'And just as good.' But now he was more careful. Whenever the white fire in the heart of the Moonstone seemed to dim in the very least, he stopped, and they took short steps this way and that, until its full brightness returned. In this way they walked slowly on until, almost before they were aware of it, so intent were they all upon the white light in the Moonstone, another white light appeared – the light of the outside world. They had reached the doorway in the knoll. They passed through, and once more they were standing on the smooth stretch of grass with the gorse and shrub before them. Borrobil reached up and withdrew his knife from the lintel of the door. And scarcely had he drawn out the knife, than the door shut, the doorway disappeared, and there was nothing before them save a grassy knoll on the side of the hill.

Yet there was this difference. Tethered to the third tree from the knoll was a shaggy pony, almost exactly like the children's ponies which were browsing peacefully near by. The pony neighed; Donald's and Jean's ponies neighed in answer. Borrobil smiled.

'One thing more has still to be done,' he said; and he pointed to the Moonstone in Donald's hand. Donald looked at it wist-fully, regretfully. Then, with a sudden movement, he flung it away. The stone made a curve of light as it sped through the air. It fell to the ground, and the ground seemed to swallow it, much as a pool swallows the pebble that is thrown in.

'So returns the Moonstone to the Fairy Queen,' said Borrobil.

But even as ripples spread out in widening circles on the surface of a pool when the pebble breaks the water's smooth face, so now ripples seemed to spread out in widening circles

on the surface of the smooth stretch of grass where the stone
had fallen. They spread out and out. They disappeared. Every
spreading ring was lost; every ring save one. One, the last ring,
still remained. Donald was puzzled and went up to it. There it
was, still clearly marked, exactly like the fairy rings he had
often seen in the meadows round the farm. 'But I'm positive
all fairy rings cannot possibly come that way,' he murmured to
himself.

CHAPTER 16

The Castle by the Sea; and
How they Met Finella there

FOR some time they had been riding northwards in silence.
Around them the high hills had gradually given way to more
open country – grassland and sandy plain. And, now, on their
right, they caught a glimpse of the sea. But what was that,
standing like a large and squat mill-chimney on the sea-coast?

'Whatever is it?' asked Donald.

'That is the castle where we should find the Princess Finella,
and also Morac and Giric,' answered Borrobil.

'A castle!' cried Jean. 'It looks a funny castle to me.'

'Yes; it may look strange to you. But as Morac told you, it
is strong and able to withstand the fiercest attacks. Nowhere
else are there castles like these, built by the Men of Orc. How
strong they are you will soon see. Yet there is one thing to
decide before we approach nearer. There must be some gift
that is offered to the castle lord. It is meet and right to come
with gifts. What is the gift you bring?'

Donald and Jean looked at one another.

'I had only my biscuits, and those I gave to King Brude,'
said Donald.

'True,' replied Borrobil. 'And there could have been no
better gift, with all that followed in its train.'

There was silence for a while.

Jean kept one hand in the pocket of her coat and there
clutched her lucky-stone. Should she offer that to the lord of
the castle? No! They had had so many adventures, and had
come so safely through them all, that surely the lucky-stone
must have had something to do with it. She couldn't give up
her lucky-stone. And in her pocket her fingers closed round

the yellow pebble and felt it lovingly. But was she being selfish?
Perhaps it was right to give up something that you wished to
keep. Perhaps Borrobil knew she had it, and was expecting her
to offer it to this lord. Then she saw that Borrobil was looking
at her. She looked straight into his eyes and said, 'I've got my
lucky-stone.'

'What that may be, I know not,' Borrobil answered. 'But it
shall be your present to the castle lord when we meet him. And
now we will approach.'

As they drew nearer to the castle they could see that it was
built of stone, broad at the base, and narrowing slightly as it
rose up in the shape of a massive round tower. Clustered near
by were a number of huts, some of stone, others of wood; and
the tower and the huts were all within a strong encircling wall
of stone. Donald gazed at the massive tower. He tried to guess
its height and its breadth. 'It's more than sixty feet high,' he
said to himself, 'for it must be more than ten times as high as
any man. And if it *is* more than sixty feet high, it must be at
least fifty feet round.' He bent his head to one side, as if that
would help him to settle the problem, and he wondered
whether, when they did real geometry at school, he would be
able to do difficult sums like working out heights and things.
Then he felt that there was something wrong with that tall
round tower. What was it? Yes! He had it! There were no
windows!

'Borrobil!' he called excitedly, 'it hasn't any windows.'

'The windows are on the inside,' answered Borrobil.

'Inside!' echoed Donald. 'Whoever heard of windows on
the inside? And how can they let in the light?'

'The tower is hollow,' Borrobil answered. 'It looks so big
because the people within it live inside the walls, and the
windows look inwards instead of outwards. But you shall see
for yourselves before very long.'

By now they had neared the strong encircling wall. They
could see a heavy gate, fast shut. But within the wall there was
no one to be seen. Borrobil reined in his pony, and held up his
hand for the children to stop too. He looked puzzled and wor-

ried. There was a frown between his eyes. Then he rode forward a short way and called.

'Hail! Friends come! Here are Borrobil and the two children.'

There was an answering hail. An old man put his head above the wall and looked at them earnestly for a long time, shading his eyes with his hand. At last he seemed satisfied. He disappeared, and they could hear him fumbling with the bars of the gate. The gate opened. They rode up and through. The old man closed the gate behind them.

Borrobil dismounted. Donald and Jean scrambled down and came to stand beside him. Clearly Borrobil was still troubled. He looked around anxiously; then he turned to the man at the gate: 'You are an old man for the duties of guard and gate-keeper,' he said, looking hard at him and still with the frown between his eyes. 'Where are the men of your lord?'

'I, only I, am left,' replied the old man.

'What mean you?' cried Borrobil. And there was something in the way he spoke that made both the children move closer to him.

'I mean what I say. Within the castle lies my lord, sick of a fever, and with him no one save the Princess Finella. The Princess, my lord, and I – we are all that are left. The strong men have gone to the fight, to the fight against the Men of the Long Ships. And with their going, the women and children have hidden themselves in the earth-houses outside the wall; for it is now known to us that the castle is no longer safe. I am here only because the man Morac, wielder of the magic sword, told us you were on your way and bade me, the oldest and weakest of us all, to stay behind, here to await your coming.'

'These are grave tidings,' answered Borrobil. 'I must see your lord at once.' And bowing slightly to the old man, he turned and walked quickly to the tower.

Donald and Jean followed anxiously. They knew there was something wrong. Finella was here, but Morac and all the men had gone to meet and to fight some unexpected foe. And why was this massive tower no longer safe? How could it be entered

anyway? There was no door. It was a broad round tower; a sheer wall of stone with not an opening anywhere. Who could capture a castle like this?

Then they saw that there *was* a door. Like the door of the outer wall it looked heavy and strong; but it was so low down, and the archway of the door was so low, that all of them would have to stoop to pass through. Borrobil was already there, and bending down to knock. He knocked hard and often, and as he knocked he called in a loud voice.

Again they heard a fumbling of the bars. The heavy door opened slowly inwards, but so slowly that it seemed to be almost too heavy to be moved. Borrobil pushed at it from the outside and it opened fully at last. He moved forward, only to step back with a start. He bowed deeply to the ground.

'Borrobil. And at your service, Princess Finella,' he said. Again he bowed deeply. 'At your service. And I fear I may be sorely needed. I came looking to find you and Morac together. But I have heard grave tidings, and I see an old man guarding the wall and a princess trying to open the castle gate. I am here to be commanded. And with me are the two stranger children, Donald and Jean.'

The Princess Finella stepped out. Now the children saw her for the first time. Jean said afterwards that she was the prettiest lady she had ever seen except her mummy. She was tall and gracious; her hair was chestnut brown with bright gleams of gold within its strands; her hazel eyes seemed to be laughing and kindly as she looked at them. But her face was serious, and there was trouble beneath those laughing kindly eyes.

'Thrice welcome, Borrobil!' she cried. 'Now are we doubly armed. The lord of the castle is within and we must take council together at once.' She turned to the children. 'And you are welcome, too. Though I would wish that you had never come. But we shall take every care of you; and, with Borrobil here, all should be well.'

She smiled at them. Donald and Jean looked shyly at her. Then Donald spoke up. 'I'm glad we're here to help,' he said.

'Yes,' added Jean. 'And I can help too.' Again the Princess smiled, and motioned to them to enter the castle. They stooped and passed through the doorway. Together Finella and Borrobil closed the heavy door and slid home the thick wooden bars that held it fast.

As their eyes grew accustomed to the half-darkness, the children saw that they were in a narrow oval chamber by the side of the door; but, beyond, there seemed to be more light, and there was also a winding flight of stone steps leading upwards. They moved hesitatingly towards the light and found themselves in an open courtyard. And at once Donald knew what Borrobil had meant when he said that the windows of the castle looked inwards and not outwards. For the castle really *was* like a chimney. Standing in the courtyard he could look straight up the chimney to a round patch of blue sky above. And dotted here and there within the inner wall of the chimney were the windows of rooms, while opening out into the courtyard where they stood he could count four doors. How queer, he thought, to live inside the walls of a chimney. But what could the old man have meant when he said that the castle was no longer safe? How could anyone capture a tall round tower with walls so thick as these; so thick that the rooms were within the walls? How could the castle be taken when its outside wall had no opening save one low doorway that could be defended by one man alone?

Jean stood silently beside him, taking it all in, and wondering about the strangeness of it all. 'It may be like a chimney, Donald,' she said, 'but it can't ever have a chimney-pot.' Donald laughed; but not easily. He was still worried. They heard Borrobil calling to them, and they moved back into the oval chamber by the door.

CHAPTER 17

In which an Army of Five Goes forth to Fight

BORROBIL and Finella were mounting the stone steps that wound upwards within the castle-walls. Donald and Jean followed. Again Donald was puzzled. The steps were lit only by the light that entered through narrow openings in the inner wall, whilst at every turn there were heavy stone slabs behind each of which he felt sure one brave man with a sword could defend the steps against a hundred. Why *was* this castle no longer safe?

They came to a landing which, as it widened slightly, became a narrow room, very similar to the room by the outer door. And at the far end of the room lay a man on some coarse rugs that had been placed on the stone floor. He was pale and thin, and his eyes burned brightly in a hollow face. As they reached him, he strove to sit up, but he was too weak and he fell back again. Borrobil moved to his side and beckoned to Jean. She came bravely forward, and taking her lucky-stone from her pocket held it out to the sick man. 'We have brought this present for you,' she said. 'I hope you will soon be better again.'

The man stretched out his hand and took the yellow pebble that Jean had long called her 'lucky-stone'. He smiled at her, and held up the pebble to his eyes. At the sight of it, he tried again to lift himself up from his rough couch, but again he fell back. He looked at Borrobil questioningly; but Borrobil shook his head.

'I knew naught of it,' said Borrobil. 'The gift was hers alone.'

The castle lord turned once more to Jean. 'The gift is of too high a price,' he said, and his voice came weakly through his lips. 'I hand it freely back. It is a bead of the choicest amber. And amber we have always treasured. But take it back. A man will do much for amber; and you may yet need it, should you need the strength and the help of a man. Take it. It is your own. Yet I thank you for offering so choice a gift.'

He held out the lucky-stone for Jean to take it back. She hesitated, for she knew that once she had given a present she should never take it back. But the sick man still held out the pebble which he had called an amber bead, and at last she allowed him to drop it into her own small hand.

Borrobil turned to Finella. 'He was ever thus,' he said. 'A noble and generous lord. But he is sadly weak. The fever has eaten far into him.'

'Yes,' she replied, 'and he frets that he is here alone, when all the rest are at the fight.'

'But I have still to hear these ill-tidings,' answered Borrobil, gravely.

'I had forgotten,' Finella said. 'Yet the tale is short enough. To the coast not far from here came five Long Ships, and the men within them landed, killing all who opposed them. Then, when the men of the neighbouring lord determined to hold his castle, which is the one that stands next to this, the invaders did not lay siege to the castle, as all expected them to do. Instead, they gathered the heather, which is now dry, and first setting fire to it, many of their number then climbed the outside wall of the castle where from the topmost height they dropped the heather in burning clumps down within the walls and into the courtyard below, always being given more and more heather as others climbed the wall and carried it up to them. And this they continued to do; nor could those within the castle put out the flames fast enough. In the end, all within were smoked out, as rats are smoked in a hole, and all were put to the sword. These tidings we had by one, who came running. Forthwith the women and children set up a loud wailing and ran to take refuge in the old earth-houses, crying out 'There we cannot be smoked alive.' But Morac and Giric, gathering together the men, went forth to meet these foes before they could march hither to attack this castle in turn. All had left but a short time before you came. And, while we await the issue of the fight, my lord here, to whom I owe so much for his great care of me, lies sick of a fever, and curses the day he cannot go forth himself to lead his men.'

'Morac is a brave man; and he has a magic sword,' said Jean quietly.

'There is much in that,' agreed Borrobil. 'Yet brave men may still be overcome by those who are too great in number.' And there was trouble in his face.

'I don't think I should like to be smoked out,' continued Jean, seriously. And she thought of what she had said about a chimney-pot. Perhaps the castle might smoke like a chimney after all.

'But can't we do something to help?' cried Donald. 'There must be something we can do. Can't your magic help us?'

Borrobil looked steadily at him. 'I must try to see where and how they fight,' he said, 'though I fear that the power of the serpent's grease on my eyes may by now have passed away. Yet perhaps it may still give me one more distant view.' He stared straight at the solid outer wall of the castle as though he were looking at one of the great stones of which it was built. So he stood for a long while, and they remained silent, watching him anxiously. At last he turned towards them. 'One last sight was granted me,' he said, 'though the vision was faint and dim. The battle rages furiously, and Morac fights like the hero all men know him to be. Giric guards his back while Morac wields valiantly the good sword Greysteel. There are many men and they fight in many groups. They fight, not on the sands, but on the raised land by the shore. The heather is dyed with blood; the strong men creep into the purple ling to breathe their last. The issue is in doubt. Yet so evenly is the battle fought that if only we could make one swift surprise on flank or rear the victory would be surely ours. Those who come to destroy should be themselves destroyed. But how can we make that swift surprise? Here, alas, my magic is of no avail.

In a great battle there is no magic to equal that of a good sword
wielded by a brave man. In battle the spear is stronger than
the charm. Here is a need of men. But where are the men we
need?'

To Borrobil's question there was no answer. There were no
men. Finella and the children stood silent. There was nothing
that they could do.

Then was the silence broken by the sick man, the lord of the
castle.

'There are indeed no men,' he said. 'But there are four brave
hearts, and there are three horses. If you are bold enough, you
may yet be enough in number.'

'Speak on,' cried Borrobil.

'This, then, can be done,' and as he spoke his purpose the
voice of the castle lord became more firm, more strong. 'You,
Borrobil, with the Princess Finella and the two children, can
take your three horses and make your way to the side of the
battle. Take with you my heavy hunting horn whose note rings
far and clear. Go to that side of the battle from which the wind
blows. Once there, quickly set light to the heather, so that the
fire may run through it and the smoke blow before you, hiding
you from the Men of the Long Ships. The heath is dry, and
the fire will run well. Then sound my horn, once, twice; and
upon the last note drive forward the horses into the smoke so
that they will neigh and panic and rush about as though there
were many horses and many men. In this way, if fortune favours
you, so the enemy may think they are surprised by another
army. At the least, they will be troubled to know what the
smoke, the note of the horn, and the sound of galloping hoofs
may mean. And in the brief anxiety that will come upon them
Morac may turn the issue of the fight and the invaders may be
overcome.'

The lord of the castle stopped. The effort had been almost
too much for him and his breath now came in short gasps. But
Borrobil still paused, irresolute. To take Finella and the
children to the very brink of the battle?

The lord of the castle read his thoughts. Once more he

spoke, but this time wearily, as one over-tired and worn out.
'No longer is my castle a safe retreat. The outer door may be
fast shut, but the outer wall can be climbed. For you and me
death matters not. We have lived our days. But the Princess
and the children are still young. Would you have them die like
rats? Even should your efforts prove unavailing, even should
the battle be lost, even should the brave Morac and all my men
be slain, you are still in the open heather, and escape, if you
wish it, may perhaps still be gained by you.'

Donald had listened to all that the sick man had said. He
felt terribly afraid, but there was something within him that
urged him on. 'We *must* go,' he cried. 'We *must* help. I'm
ready now.'

'And you know I said that I would help, too,' added Jean,
and her small voice sounded strangely serious.

Finella looked anxiously at them. Her eyes were grave and
sad. Then she seemed to make up her mind. 'It is perhaps
better so,' she said. 'There is no other way.' And having said
that, she smiled at them, a smile half wistful, half encouraging.
She seized Jean and kissed her tenderly. To Donald she held
out her hand. 'You are both brave children,' she added, and
there was nothing better she could have said.

Borrobil nodded, and his nod seemed to mean approval of
everything: of the plan, of Finella's decision, and of her words
to the children.

'And the fire-sticks?' he asked. The sick lord raised his hand
and pointed to a niche in the wall. Borrobil stepped to the niche
and reaching up took from it what looked to Donald like two
pieces of wood. These he tucked within his belt.

'We shall do what we can,' he said gravely, and with that
he led the way out of the room and down the stone steps to the
castle door. The others followed him. Once more the bars were
slid back; together Finella and Borrobil pulled open the heavy
door. Outside the castle Jean and Donald mounted their own
shaggy ponies. The Princess Finella was given the pony that
the fairies had lent to Borrobil. Borrobil walked. They came
to the gate of the encircling wall and the old man whom Morac

had posted there as guard and gate-keeper stepped forward to open the gate.

'We go to the fight,' cried Borrobil. 'Will you join us and be on our side?'

The old man looked at them, unbelievingly. Then he saw that Borrobil's face was grim, and that the faces of Finella and the children were set and serious.

''Tis a strange army,' he said. 'But I can still add one to its number.' And opening wide the gate he walked shoulder to shoulder with Borrobil.

CHAPTER 18

How the Army Fought and Won; and How One of its Number was Lost

THERE was a confused sound of the clash of sword and axe on helm and shield. As the battle swayed to and fro, so the sound came nearer or moved away. Once or twice Donald half expected to see armed men fighting over and around him; but he set his lips tight and determined that he, one-fifth of the new army, would do his best. He wondered whether the noise they were to make would be heard; whether their plan would succeed. And what if the smoke simply rolled over the fight and nothing more? But he was surprised that the battle was not louder. 'Perhaps they have no more breath to shout with,' he thought to himself; and he was right. He glanced for a moment at Jean, hiding in a hollow behind a large patch of heather. He noticed that her small face was determined; her eyes bright; and that she was gripping tightly the bunch of dry grass that Borrobil had given her in readiness for the fire. Then he looked back again to Borrobil.

They were at their battle-stations. Borrobil had given them their orders. Each knew what to do and how to do it; what heather and grass to set alight, how to keep behind the smoke, and how to shout.

Borrobil glanced around, taking in the position of his tiny force. Then calling the old gate-keeper to his side he bent down and pulled out of his belt the fire-sticks. Donald crept closer to see what Borrobil was going to do. One of the fire-sticks seemed to be a flat piece of wood and nothing more. But the other was round and long, with a pointed end, rather like a wooden meat-skewer, except that it was somewhat thicker and had a queer flat top to it that made it look like an overgrown

mushroom. Then he saw Borrobil fit the pointed end of the
'mushroom's' stalk into a hole in the flat piece of wood while
the old gate-keeper put his hand on the flat top of the 'mushroom' and by pressing hard upon it so pressed the point firm
and true within the hole. And now Borrobil took out a thin
leather thong. This he passed twice round the 'mushroom's'
stalk and then, holding the ends of the thong one in each hand,

he pulled each end rapidly in turn. Round and round, first this
way, then that, span the pointed stick in the hole in the wood;
harder and harder pressed the old gate-keeper so that the point
bit deep into the hole. A minute passed; two minutes; three
minutes. Still Borrobil span the fire-stick. And then, suddenly,
Donald saw a thin wisp of smoke rising from the hole in the
wood. For a brief space Borrobil seemed to spin even faster;
and Donald thought he caught a glimpse of a dull glow at the

meeting place of the two pieces of wood. Quickly Borrobil
bent down and blew. A flame flickered. Again Borrobil blew;
and this time he thrust a thin bunch of dry grass into the hole
in the wood. A new and stronger wisp of grey smoke puffed
out. Once more Borrobil blew; and the bunch of grass was
alight. 'So have we our need-fire,' he cried softly; and with
that he thrust the burning grass into the heather before
him.

Donald had watched all with amazement, but now the
burning heather stirred him to action. He remembered his
orders. Quickly he stepped forward and thrust his own bunch
of dry grass into the burning heather, so setting it alight, and
then ran outwards again to start in another place new fires of
his own. Jean and Finella ran up and did likewise. Now all of
them ran in a line, up and down, thrusting bunches of burning
grass into the heather and dry growth, shouting as they ran.
But always they kept to the hollows, so that they were not seen.
Only the billowing smoke could be seen as it rose in the air
and began to roll across the heath towards the battle. Soon
the fires, caught by the wind, were joining one another. The
smoke became a great cloud, and behind it they raised shout
after shout. Then Borrobil put the horn to his mouth. He blew
a long note, sharp and clear. He took a deep breath, and again
the horn sent out its ringing all over the land. As soon as the
second call had died away, Finella, Borrobil, and the old man
each seized a pony by its bridle and began to lead it into the
smoke. The ponies reared and whinnied; one of them gave a
long neigh. Into the smoke they were pulled rather than led,
and once well within the burning heath they were let loose.
They made a great noise, neighing and whinnying; they galloped wildly backwards and forwards to escape from the smoke
and the fires that licked their hoofs. The smoke rolled on. The
army of five gave one united shout. They had fulfilled their
task. There was nothing more that they could do.

Jean felt suddenly tired. She crept away from the others and
sat down by a small birch tree. She thought of the smoke, the
noise, the fight. By now the battle had been lost or won. What

would happen to them if all their efforts had failed to help
Morac to win? Would they still escape in the heather? But
what was that? She heard a sound behind her. She started to
her feet, and found herself looking at a tall man with fair hair
and blue eyes and with a queer wing-shaped helmet on his
head. On his left arm he carried a shield, and she saw that
there were dents in it. At his side a long sword was hanging
from his belt. For a moment he seemed as startled as Jean.
Then his eyes hardened, and his mouth suddenly looked cruel.
He bent down quickly; he picked her up, tucked her roughly
under his right arm and made off across the heather and away
from the sea. She cried out, 'Borrobil! Borrobil!' but no one
seemed to hear. And at her very first cry the man squeezed her
so tightly under his arm that he took her breath away and it
was difficult to cry out at all. He was squeezing her so tightly
that she felt hurt all over. She was terrified. Soon she was
sobbing bitterly.

None of the others had seen or heard. They had watched the
smoke rolling across the dry heath; they had heard and seen
the ponies run back out of the smoke and the low licking flames.
But no one saw or heard Jean. All of them were too engrossed
with the success or failure of their efforts. Borrobil had crept
forward to see what was happening on the field of battle; and
Finella, Donald, and the old gate-keeper were staring intently
ahead awaiting his return. Now he came running back.

'They are taking to their ships,' he cried. 'They are sailing
away. The battle is won. Come! We will join the victors. We
will praise Morac, Giric, all of them, for their noble fight. And
we shall tell them, too, of the army of five that made its own
attack in the very nick of time.' He grinned merrily at them.
Then his grin seemed to stand still and melt from his face.

'Jean?' he cried. 'Where is Jean?'

No one seemed to know.

'I'm sure she's all right,' said Donald. 'I saw her sitting
down somewhere not so long ago. But I can't remember
exactly where. It was after the smoke and the ponies, so she
must be all right.'

But Borrobil was not satisfied. 'We must find her,' he said. 'We must look at once.'

They began their search, at first perhaps a little half-heartedly, soon earnestly, then frantically. Jean was not to be found. Before long Morac came up to them. 'I knew I should find you here,' he called happily to Borrobil. 'No sooner had I seen the smoke and heard the call of the horn than I knew who had come to our aid. And now they have fled, leaving two of their ships which they have no longer the men to man. But what seek you? Why this turning hither and thither behind every bush and tree like a child at a game?' He spoke crossly; and now on his face could be seen the dry sweat of the battle and he moved wearily as one utterly worn out. Borrobil looked up at him. 'Jean,' he answered. 'We were an army of five, and one of our army is lost.'

'Five?' queried Morac, following Borrobil as he moved quickly about looking here and here. 'Five?'

'Yes, five,' answered Borrobil tersely. 'The Princess Finella, Donald, Jean, the old keeper of the gate, and I. All of us had equal share in the victory. And now Jean is lost. But this is no time for talk or tale. You must help us to find her. Bring here all those who can still walk that they may help us in the search. Jean must be found.'

Morac walked heavily back to the scene of the fight. This was bad news after good. But surely no evil could have befallen her. She was bound to be lying somewhere, weary and worn-out with the excitements and adventures she had had. She would soon be found. Suddenly he stopped. The strange look once more came into his face and he passed his hand over his eyes. He stumbled as he ran back.

'Borrobil!' he called. 'The dragon's skin! I saw Jean standing in a hollow by the side of Giric who lay stretched upon the ground. Two men of the Long Ships also lay stretched beside him. And Jean held something in her hand.'

'Giric!' cried Borrobil. 'But Giric is with *you*.'

Finella and Donald joined them. No words were passed. They moved as quickly as they could towards the field of battle, and the men who had fought there so valiantly so shortly before. Some were lying full length upon the ground; others were sitting in small groups. Out to sea three long ships were sailing away from the land. Two other ships were drawn up on the beach below.

'Giric!' they called. 'Where is Giric?'

But no one had seen Giric; and Giric was nowhere to be seen.

CHAPTER 19

Two Shoes and Two Men; and How
Jean Found a Use for Her
'Lucky-Stone'

THE man stopped. He put Jean down on the ground beside him, and leant back against a tree. He was breathing heavily. Jean looked at him, miserably. She was sore and frightened. There was nothing to do but to lie still and wait to be carried away again. What was this man going to do with her? He couldn't be going to kill her or he would have done it at once. Why had he carried her away like this? Perhaps she could still escape? Perhaps he would go to sleep and she could crawl away? But where could she go?

She sat up, carefully, for her arms and sides were bruised and ached. The man was still leaning against the tree. Every now and then he looked around. Was he looking to see if they had been followed? Or was he expecting someone to meet him? She saw that they had come to a narrow pass very similar to that through which she had ridden with Donald, Borrobil, Morac, and Giric. That was all over, now. She had liked Borrobil and Morac. Borrobil was a clever man, and sometimes he was funny. Morac was brave, and he had a magic sword. She was happy then, even though she had been a little frightened when she was a prisoner in Sulig's castle, and even perhaps a little frightened when she knew that Grugol was hiding behind the big stone at the head of the pass. But then Borrobil and Morac had been with her. But had they? Borrobil wasn't with her when she and Donald were lifted up in the mist. He had come specially to rescue them. Perhaps Borrobil and Morac would both come to rescue her this time! The thought cheered her for a while. And this man could never fight Morac; while Borrobil could easily turn him into a snake or something. Of course they would come!

A stone that had been knocked loose on the hill at the side of the pass came rattling down. She started. So did the man. He put his hand to his sword and moved his shield round in front of him. So he stood alert for a brief space. Then, all at once, he held up his hand in greeting, and Jean saw another man, also wearing a queer wing-shaped helmet, come striding down the side of the hill to join him. 'Hail! Ketil,' he said. 'I saw you come this way when we parted. Think you that we may yet get away in one of the two ships that are left on the beach?' His eyes caught Jean and he came closer. 'But what have you here?' he asked.

'I know not,' replied the man called Ketil. 'Dearly would I like to know. She is too heavy by far for a fairy or an elf. And yet never saw I human child dressed like that. 'Tis a queer dress.'

Somehow, Jean had never thought about the strange clothes everyone else had worn ever since she and Donald had first met Borrobil; but now her own clothes did seem rather funny.

'A queer dress, as you say,' answered the newcomer. 'But she is a human child all the same. Though she may be a changeling, perhaps. They do grow heavy; heavier than other children. Has this one spoken? A changeling never speaks to be understood.'

'Hardly would you call it speaking,' replied Ketil, 'though indeed she yelled hard enough when I picked her up. Some sort of odd name she called, or it may be she spoke in a foreign tongue. I cannot say.'

'Well, it would be easy to tell if she were a changeling had we but twenty-four egg-shells handy. Those we could place in a ring, and then tell her we were about to boil water in them. That, they say, is a sure test. Always then, they say, a change- ling will cry out that it has lived with the fairies for hundreds of years but never yet has it seen water boiled in egg-shells laid in a ring. And then is it known for a changeling without doubt.' He paused reflectively. 'But we have no egg-shells. What shall

you do with her? Shall we run a sword through her and move on? I know this country from our last raid. If we take this track up the pass there is an old hill-fort at the head of it. We could hide there for a while.'

'Good,' said Ketil. 'We will take to the fort. And I shall take the child also. Changeling or not, there may be a heavy ransom for her. Perhaps she is the child of some great man who would pay heavily in much gold to have her back. Who knows?'

' "He who fights should bear no burden" is a true saying,' said the other. 'But if you think there may be a ransom, the burden may be worth the bearing. For myself, I've fought enough for one day. How many think you were those who drove the smoke before them as they came to the aid of Morac and his men?'

'Doubtless it was a large band,' answered Ketil, 'and we were fortunate to escape; but unfortunate that the man Morac with his sword stood between us and the ships.'

(Jean felt cheered a little at that. 'A large band,' she thought, 'and there were only five of us.' And these men were still afraid of Morac and his sword.)

'But we must move on.'

'Even so.'

Again the man called Ketil lifted Jean up under his arm, though this time he carried her more easily. Then, his companion leading the way, they moved on slowly, taking the track that led upward through the pass.

For a long time they walked in silence, until suddenly, Jean heard Ketil call out, 'What lies in the way? What have you found?'

'Only a shoe,' called back his companion from some distance ahead. 'And a good shoe at that. But of what use is one shoe to a man who has two feet? Had I its fellow then indeed should I be lucky. But never was I the lucky one. There it goes.'

Jean heard the shoe make a soft thud, and guessed that the man had thrown it aside.

Once more fear clutched at her heart. Perhaps Morac and

Borrobil would never come. Perhaps these men would hide
with her until they could carry her over the sea to a strange
land so that she would never see Donald again. And all the time
she was being carried further and further away from the castle,
Finella, Borrobil, everyone. Her small face began to pucker;
and just as the tears were about to fall, again she heard the
man in front call out – 'Hold! What have we here? Another
shoe. And by mighty Thor 'tis the fellow of that which I threw
away but a short time past. I should have a fine pair were I to
go back to fetch that first one. And that I will. Await me. For
once, it is I who am the lucky one.'

Jean saw his legs as he ran past Ketil and down the path the
way they had come. She could hear him still running in the
distance, his steps growing fainter and fainter. She wondered
if he would find the shoe he had thrown away, and as she
wondered, suddenly, to her surprise, the man Ketil jumped,
and put her hastily to the ground. She heard a voice, a voice
she recognized. It cried 'Run, Jean.'

Quickly she picked herself up, and there saw Giric with
sword and shield, facing the man Ketil. She ran to the side of
the pass and crept behind a large stone. Soon she heard their
swords clash. Blow met blow. Sword rang on shield; sword
met sword. But she dared not watch. She hid her eyes with both
hands, and kept saying and saying, 'O Giric, do win! do win!'
Once she wondered why Giric had come and not Morac.
Morac with his magic sword would have killed this hateful
man with one blow. But could Giric win? 'O Giric, do win! do
win!'

As they fought, their breath came in sharp gasps. But now
came a sharper gasp, followed by a cry, and by a crash as one
of them fell to the ground. Who had fallen? Did she dare to
look? Slowly and fearfully she took her hands from her eyes
and peeped over the stone. A wave of gladness swept through
her, and she felt she wanted to cry again. For there stood Giric,
erect and stern; but the man Ketil lay full length upon the
ground. 'One,' said Giric shortly. 'And here comes the other.'

Jean looked, and saw Ketil's companion returning up the

path. Already he had drawn his sword, and he was walking
warily, 'exactly like a cat', she thought, 'when it is trying to
catch a bird it has seen on the grass'. In his left hand the man
carried a pair of shoes, but as he drew nearer he put them down
carefully by the side of the path. Jean wondered about those
shoes. Where had they come from? A thought struck her. She
looked at Giric's feet. He was wearing no shoes!

And now began the second fight. Again Jean hid her eyes as
again she heard the sound of sword on shield. This time she
thought the fight would never end. On and on they fought;
she heard them moving this way and that; she heard them grunt
as blow followed blow. 'O do win, Giric! Do win!' she repeated
time after time. But still they fought. She heard a sharp cry
of pain. Was that Giric? Immediately it was followed by a
louder cry and a heavy crash. And upon that, another crash,
another cry. Then all was quiet.

Terrified, Jean crept out from behind her stone. This time
Giric no longer stood erect and stern. He lay stretched upon
the ground, and beside him lay his second foe. For a moment,
she stood still, dazed and frightened. Then, quickly, she ran to
Giric's side. As she reached him he raised himself slightly and
smiled at her, that old twisted smile of his.

'Both,' he said. 'And no scratch upon me. But the ribs in
my side are broken and one ankle at least is no good to me.
When you take to fighting, Jean, fight with your shoes on.' The
thought seemed to amuse him, for he smiled again and looked
at her with something like a twinkle in his eye. 'And now when
I could get my shoes back again, I don't need them any more.
For I shall have to be carried like a sack of meal on a man's
back.'

'I will get someone to carry you,' said Jean.

'How?' asked Giric quietly.

'I don't know,' she answered. 'But I shall run and look for
someone, and then we can all go back to the castle again. I
would belift you myself if I could.'

'I'm sure you would,' he said, gently.

Jean looked round. The path, the hill-side, everywhere

seemed deserted. Where should she go? How could she find someone and make him come to Giric? Then she thought of her lucky-stone. The sick man in the castle had said something about it when he gave it back to her. Hadn't he said that it was amber, and that any man would do a lot for her if she gave it to him? She knew the castle man had said something like that. She took the amber bead out of her pocket and looked at it in her hand. Then she turned to Giric.

'I shall find someone and give him my bead to carry you,' she said.

CHAPTER 20

A Triumphant Return

'OH, dear,' said Jean to herself, 'I *am* tired. I know I can't climb those steep sides, and my legs feel worn out. I will follow the path and then I can't lose my way when I come back with someone.'

She followed the path as it wound its way between the hills; and although she felt bruised, weary and unhappy, she pushed bravely on. And fortune favoured her; for she had not been walking long when she saw a wisp of blue smoke curling upwards at the side of the pass. She tried to run, but found she couldn't; the best she could do was a kind of half-walk, half-stumble. 'Oh, I *am* wearisome, ' she said to herself.

But every step was a step nearer. Nearer and nearer. Would she find anyone there? Yes! Someone had been watching her! She was certain she saw someone moving away as she approached. Yet that was funny! For here was a man sitting idly by a fire of blazing wood that burned brightly in a kind of hearth made out of a circle of flat stones. He looked as though he had been there for ages; he never even moved as she stumbled forward. Was he just pretending, and had he been watching her all along? She stood in front of him. 'Please,' she cried breathlessly, 'please, I want you to carry Giric.'

The man still sat there, and made no sign.

'Oh, please,' she cried, 'you must help me.'

Still the man sat silent. Then –

'Who's Giric?' he asked, so suddenly and sharply that she jumped back.

'Oh, he's hurt in the pass, and he can't walk, and you must help him.'

'Not me,' answered the man. 'He who keeps out of the fight keeps a whole skin.'

'But they stopped fighting long ago, and you must help,' pleaded Jean.

'That's as may be. They stop fighting; I stop here.'

Jean looked at him. There was still her lucky-stone. Perhaps that would make him come. She put her hand in her pocket and pulled it out.

'But you won't stop here if I give you my lucky-stone, will you?' she asked, holding it out to him.

The man jumped to his feet so quickly that again he startled her. 'Amber!' he cried. 'I'd go for that any day!' He stopped, and a queer look came into his eyes. 'But as you've brought it to me I needn't go for it, need I?' he added.

Jean suddenly felt afraid. Did he mean he'd just take her lucky-stone from her and still do nothing to help Giric? The man saw her fear, and his look gradually changed. 'It's as well you found me,' he said. 'Not for nothing am I called "Honest Haff". Give me the bead and I'll serve you as best I may.'

She handed the bead to him, still wondering a little whether he was as honest as he said. He looked at it for a long time, turning it this way and that in his hand. Then he looked at Jean. 'Well hid is never found,' he said. 'Go back to the man Giric, and I will follow you.'

'But you don't know where Giric is,' she cried.

'I can see your back a long way off,' was his answer, 'but your back has no eyes to see where I shall put the bead.'

Jean knew what he meant. Slowly she began to make her way down to the path again, and almost at once the man had joined her. Again he looked queerly at her, and even while she was wondering what his look could mean he said in a quiet voice, 'You are tired. And you are a brave child. Shall I carry you a little way?'

'Please,' she said. 'I think you are nice now.' And soon she felt suddenly all comfortable and happy and relieved as the man lifted her up in his arms and strode down the pass.

The return to the place where Giric lay seemed no distance at all. The man put Jean gently down and spoke to Giric, asking about his hurt, how best he could be carried, and whither

he was to carry him. Soon, with surprising ease, he had lifted
Giric on to his back, and with Jean walking at his side they
were on their way to the castle, and to Donald, Borrobil, and
Morac.

Meantime at the castle all rejoicing over the enemy's defeat
and rout had changed to sadness and gloom. It was as though
a black cloud had suddenly covered the bright summer sun.
Borrobil and Morac paced to and fro outside the tall tower.
From time to time Borrobil would call himself 'an old fool'
for failing to keep an eye on Jean, and for failing to bring with
him his small jar of serpent's grease so that he could renew his
power of distant sight and see all that was happening to her
afar off. Morac, no less worried, often put his hand to the sword
Greysteel; but what was the use of a magic sword when the
enemy was out of reach and unknown? Within the tower itself,
Finella had taken Donald into one of the rooms, where she
tried vainly to talk of other things. But the boy kept asking
about Jean; and there was nothing Finella could say beyond a
vague and oft-repeated assurance that all would be well and
that Jean was sure to come back again, safe and sound, before
very long. The sick lord had been lifted from his rough couch
and carried down to the castle door, so that there, as he said,
he might be with those who sorrowed, and yet also be there
the sooner to hear the glad news that all was well.

And soon the glad news came, its messenger the old gate-
keeper from the outer wall. He came running.

'What has thou seen?' cried Morac, rushing to meet him.

'A man, carrying another on his back.'

'And the maid?'

'Alas! there is no sign of the maid.'

Borrobil and Morac rushed to the gate in the wall. They
rushed through the gate and across the heath. And there they
met Giric being carried 'like a sack of meal on a man's
back'.

'And Jean?' they cried anxiously.

'Take me, Morac, on to that broad back of thine, and this
good man shall return for Jean,' answered Giric. 'The maid is

worn out and weary, and could no longer walk. She lies peace-fully in the heather waiting to be brought in in triumph.'

But Morac was of another mind. Hastily he inquired where in the heather he would find her, and then, bidding the man carry Giric safely to the castle, he himself went out to carry in the valiant Jean.

And so, within the briefest space, the black cloud had rolled away and the sun shone brightly again. Giric, lying within the first room by the doorway to the castle, told how, at the very close of the battle, he had seen one of the men of the Long Ships fleeing into the country and away from the boats; how, in following him, he had seen him pick up Jean and carry her off; how, later, the first man had been joined by a second, so that now he feared he could not fight both of them and so save Jean. Then he had remembered the old trick whereby one man might divide two and so fight them one at a time. If he could only get ahead of them he might use his own shoes for a like purpose. 'So, hastily making my way behind the hills I reached the track in the pass unseen and in front of them,' he concluded, 'and the trick worked. The man who was leading the way found first my one shoe and then the other. He went back to recover the first shoe, and thus was I able to fight, first the man who was carrying Jean, and then his companion. But in fighting the second man, just as my sword drove through his helm so that he fell lifeless to the ground, even at that very moment did I catch my foot on a stone. The pain seemed to numb me to the thigh; my foot twisted and down I went, almost on top of him, and across his shield which was standing half-upright on its edge beside him. My side struck hard on the edge of the shield, and in that way all the ribs in my side were broken. With a twisted ankle and broken ribs, I could not walk. Then it was that the maid went bravely out to seek for help. Help she found and brought to me. And here we are, and here she is.'

'Never were there braver tales to tell,' cried Borrobil. 'An army of five that puts the foe to flight; an army of two children, a princess and two old men; a man who fights shoeless to rescue a maid; and a maid who rescues her rescuer. These are stirring deeds. I must sing of them.'

'A song! Borrobil, a song!' they cried; and Jean, to show that she was now fully her old self again, clapped her hands and came running to stand beside him.

> '*With smoke and wild horses, with horn and with cry,*
> *An army of five faced the foe;*
> *Two children, Finella, an old man and I*
> *Set light to the heather where wild the winds blow.*

> '*With smoke and wild horses we carried the day,*
> *The foemen made haste in their going;*
> *But one of our army was carried away,*
> *Fast burns the heather the wild winds are blowing.*

> '*Seized by the foemen so swiftly they bore her*
> *Far from their ships by the sea;*
> *But Giric has followed them, challenged them, fought for her,*
> *Wild blows the wind as the heather burns free.*

> '*Deep in the heather boldly went five of us,*
> *Morac and Giric stood fast in the fight;*
> *Giric the shoeless brought one back alive to us,*
> *Fierce blows the wind in the heather alight.*

> '*Sing loud the praises of Morac the peerless,*
> *One agèd gate-keeper, two children fearless,*
> *Giric the shoeless, Finella the fair;*
> *Where fierce burns the heather*
> *There all strove together,*
> *Doing and daring so valiantly there.*'

Loud shouts of approval rang out as Borrobil ended his song. But now Morac had moved over to Finella and was standing by her side. Borrobil saw this with eyes that were again bright and mischievous. He saw, too, that the time had come for their going. Turning to the lord of the castle on his rough couch by the door, he made one of his deep bows, and said, 'And now must we set forth on our return journey. We came for the Princess Finella whom you have cared for so truly and so well.

Now she returns with us to her father's kingdom, there to be welcomed by a people set free from the dragon's thrall, and there to be married to the brave and noble Morac. To you, my lord,' continued Borrobil, 'to you I would offer the deepest thanks of my master, King Brude, and of all his Council for the loving care with which you have safeguarded our Princess.'

'Enough,' interrupted the castle lord; 'I deemed it an honour to serve, and the Princess Finella has been a comfort and a joy to all of us.'

'All who know her know that that will always be said of her,' answered Borrobil, and this time his sweeping bow took in Finella, the castle lord, Morac, everyone; and the white owl's feather in the tip of his hat bobbed up and down excitedly as if to say that it, too, agreed with every word.

'True,' replied the sick lord, 'true indeed. But lovers are impatient of delay. Let Morac and his princess ride back to their own kingdom. To King Brude I send my greetings and the greetings of the Men of Orc. Tell him we have known no warrior to equal Morac, no sword the match of Greysteel, no princess like unto Finella, no children like unto the two stranger children who came with you, and last, but not least, no one to equal Borrobil. Delay no longer. May you fare well.' And the castle lord smiled at Borrobil who, for once, could find no words in reply; the best he could do was to bow again and to grin happily, while this time it looked to the children as though the white owl's feather, moving slowly up and down, was feeling fully as embarrassed as Borrobil.

All the men of the castle now gathered round the small group as it prepared for the return journey, each man offering what help he could.

'Need we go back the way we came?' asked Donald. 'Can't we sail back in one of the two ships that are on the beach? I'd love to sail back in a ship.'

'Oh yes,' cried Jean eagerly, 'I love ships and boats; I love sailing ships and oaring boats, I love all of them.'

Borrobil looked at Morac and Finella. The two of them looked at one another, and Finella nodded her head.

'The journey would be no longer,' said Morac, 'and Finella would take delight in pleasing the children.'

'But the Blue Men?' said Borrobil, questioningly.

'True,' answered Morac, and now there was doubt in his voice. 'I had forgotten the Blue Men. That is a danger greater than any that could come to us by land. It would be better for the children's safety if we were to make our way back through the mountain pass again.'

'Oh no!' cried Donald and Jean together. 'We *must* go in the boat. Morac will look after us and will fight the Blue Men with his sword, won't you Morac?'

Morac shook his head and looked anxiously at Borrobil. He knew full well that against the Blue Men his courage and his sword would be of no avail.

But Borrobil returned his look and smiled. 'With the knowledge I have of the Blue Men's ways, surely we can be ready for the worst that they may try to do. But you will have to trust me.'

'Of our trust there can be no doubt,' replied Morac gravely, 'and a meeting with the Blue Men would be a meeting worth remembering.'

CHAPTER 21

The Blue Men: How they Met them, How they Escaped from them, and How a Gift was Given in Time of Need

THE ship was a good ship. She rode the seas easily, her prow rising and falling with the waves. There was a steady 'flap, flap' as the waters ran past her sides, while from above came an occasional answering 'flup, flup' as the sail bellied in the wind. At the helm sat Borrobil, looking like a sailor born and bred who had sailed the seven seas and knew all that a sailor should.

The children were delighted. They hung over the sides, dipping their hands in the water or watching the white spray breaking from the sharp prow. But Donald was still thinking over the talk between Morac and Borrobil just before they had sailed. There was something he wanted to know; and at last he could wait no longer.

'Who are the Blue Men, Borrobil?' he asked. 'And why are they dangerous?'

'They are the men of the sea,' replied Borrobil; 'and the men of the sea are always dangerous to those who put their trust in ships.'

'Men of the sea!' cried Jean.

'Yes,' answered Borrobil, simply. 'In the waters of the narrow strait through which we shall have to pass, and which we are now nearing, there live the Blue Men of whom all sailors are afraid. Their home is the water as our home is the land. Sometimes in summer they may be seen swimming lightly just below the surface of the sea; and then are they to be known by their grey faces and by the blue caps they wear. But in winter, when the sea is cold, then do they throw themselves about, splashing and tumbling to keep themselves warm, so that hardly can they be seen amid the fury of the waves. Yet in so doing, often will their arms raise the waves to such a height that no ship can live in the sea.'

'But that's only a story,' said Donald, knowingly. 'Why should the Blue Men have anything to do with it? Everybody knows that the sea is calm in summer and rough in winter.'

'And that may be true, also,' admitted Borrobil. 'Yet often the Blue Men will attack a ship even in the calm of summer. And that they will do for cruel sport, seizing hold of it with their strong arms and pulling it below the waves so that all within it are drowned. For a time the sailor may see them swimming lightly around, then, suddenly, he will find his ship in direst peril from their grip. Amid huge waves they will turn to dash upon his craft; in their strong arms they will seize his boat, and try to drag it down to the lowest deep.'

'Oh, I do hope they won't come near this boat,' said Jean, a little fearfully. 'I'm sure the sea is much more ruggledy than it was.'

Donald looked out across the waves, and his heart began to beat more quickly. Certainly the sea had become much rougher, so that the prow of the ship was now mounting higher and higher in the rollers; certainly the wind had begun to make strange noises in the sail. Suddenly he heard Jean call out –

'Borrobil! I saw the arms of the Blue Men!'

Then Donald felt Morac put his arm round him. He saw that Finella was holding Jean. He saw that Borrobil was smiling at them, and that there was a queer dancing light in his eyes.

'Yes, the Blue Men,' said Borrobil quietly. 'But there is one certain way to make them loosen their grip. Before long one of them will rise from the sea. He will seize the prow and call out to us. He will call out the first two lines of a verse. Then must I add the two last lines on the very instant. This he will do three times. Three times must I finish his verse for him. If

I succeed in so doing, then shall we be no more troubled and the sea will again become calm.'

Donald felt relieved. After all hadn't Borrobil answered the three riddles of the Fairy Queen? But what a queer world this was! Three riddles in verses. Now three verses to be completed. Three magic tests with Sulig. Yes! And three biscuits and nine-standing-stones! 'Three threes are nine.' Why *was* everything in threes? He looked at Jean. She seemed to be all right, and Finella was rubbing Jean's cheek up against her own. Finella was a lovely princess. When he grew up he'd like to fight for a princess like Finella. But how rough the sea was! And the waves were mounting higher and higher.

Morac's grip round him tightened. Donald felt the prow of the ship going down, down, down into a deep trough. The ship quivered; it seemed to shake itself; and a voice rang out:

> *'What are the words, O Borrobil!*
> *That will save your ship in our sea?'*

But Borrobil was ready. Quickly came his answer, shouted above the roar of the wind and the waves:

> *'My good ship answers her master's will;*
> *And her course is laid by me.'*

Morac gave a grunt. The prow was riding the waves again. Up, crash, splash, over, down, up, up, crash, splash, over, down. Donald looked at Borrobil. He was actually grinning as he swung on the helm! 'One,' he cried, cheerfully.

But the ship was still plunging heavily. Still it looked as though every wave would engulf them. Finella looked at Morac, and he smiled back at her. Jean saw the smile. She looked at Borrobil and saw that he was smiling too. What was there to be frightened of? But scarcely had the new feeling of security come upon her, than again the ship gave a heavy plunge; again it shivered along its whole length; its timbers seemed to crack. And again the voice rang out:

> *'Our arms are ready, our arms are strong;*
> *Why should you sail our sea?'*

Every eye turned to Borrobil. He took one hand from the helm and holding it to his mouth shouted aloud his reply:

> *'My ship is steady, my ship is strong;*
> *Brave hearts are here with me.'*

And as if in immediate response to him, the ship did seem to run more steadily. He nodded his head saucily, and called out 'Two!' But almost at once Morac gave another and a different cry.

'Look! A Long Ship!'

Donald looked up; so did Finella and Jean. There, in the distance, was a Long Ship similar to the one they were now sailing. Like them it was running before the wind. But was it following them because it could follow no other course? Or was it pursuing them?

Borrobil watched it for a few moments. He cried fiercely, 'They shall never take us!' Then his face lightened and his eyes shone. He looked at Jean. 'Now shall your own gift from the Fairy Queen be ours,' he called, 'and this our time of greatest need shall be their time of greatest peril.' And quickly he turned once more to tend the helm.

Now the sea became rougher and more tumultuous than ever before. Every board in the ship seemed to groan aloud. The waves seemed to rush upon them as though determined to bear them down mercilessly by sheer weight. The mighty rollers loomed high above their prow. Sometimes, in a trough of the sea, they appeared to be caught between two high hills of towering deep green water. The ship plunged and reared, or heeled over first to one side and then to the other. But Borrobil kept her head to the waves. His eyes were bright and keen, and always a smile played round his mouth as though he took delight in the roaring madness of the vast waters.

And then, as they plunged deep into a hollow between two mountainous waves, then, once more, the voice rang out:

> *'What do you seek that you come our way?*
> *What does your coming mean?'*

And immediately Borrobil's answering shout was heard:

> '*We look for the gift of the white sea-spray,*
> *Vouchsafed by the Fairy Queen.*'

'Three!' cried Borrobil; and as he cried out, so Jean remembered. A gift in time of need! The Fairy Queen had promised her a gift of the white sea-spray in their time of greatest need. But how could the white sea-spray help them amid all these mighty waves? And even if they escaped the dangers of the sea, how could the white spray save them from the men of the pursuing ship?

Yet scarcely had Borrobil completed the verse, than the waves seemed to be less violent, less fearful. The ship seemed to ride the waters more easily. But also as the sea grew less tumultuous, so the air grew heavier, and more oppressive. Large drops of rain began to fall, at first slowly, then faster and faster. The rain stopped. But still the air was heavy, so that they seemed to be weighed down with it; they felt as though soon they would be gasping for breath. For the briefest moment all seemed quiet in an unexpected calm, when suddenly there came a hissing noise, threatening, terrifying. It grew louder and louder. Then the noise seemed to move away from them, only to turn again, so that now it seemed to be all around them, as though they were in the centre of a multitude of aerial fiends shrieking and tearing their wild course through the heavens. Again, the fearful sound seemed to move away; and Morac cried out: 'Look!'

He pointed to the sea behind them. There rode the Long Ship. It was still some distance away. But it was not to the ship that Morac pointed. Near that pursuing ship the sea appeared to be bulging up as though a strange hill of water was rising from its midst, while over the ship itself a large black cloud hovered like some bird of evil omen. Then, as they watched, they saw a long column of water like a thickly twisted rope reach out from the cloud and stretch downward towards the sea, always moving this way and that as if it were groping for that strangely rising hill in the midst of the waves. The column

of water from the cloud above twisted and whirled; the hill
of water in the sea beneath seemed to move to join it. At
last they met. A mighty column of angry water joined
sea and cloud together. And there within that wild mad
meeting of the elements, there plunged the pursuing Long
Ship.

And now the sea grew white with spray. The spray ran up
and round the dark column of angry water as it whirled between cloud and sea. Higher and higher danced the white sea-
spray as it climbed the column towards the cloud above. Almost
had it reached the cloud when suddenly, strangely, sea and
cloud were again apart. No longer were they joined by that
twisted pillar of angry water. The white spray seemed to rush
tumultuously down to rejoin the sea where now it played
hither and thither on the crests of the turbulent waves. But
the Long Ship had gone! Deep beneath the dancing spray the
Blue Men claimed their spoil.

For long all were silent. Then Borrobil spoke. 'So were we
given the white sea-spray in our time of greatest need,' he said
quietly. 'Once, in the midst of the storm, I thought it might
be given to hide us from the pursuing foe; little did I think it
would be given in the mad tumult of the water-spout.'

Donald and Jean looked back to where, from the storm-
cloud above, the whirling funnel of water had hung down to
join the rising sea beneath. There the waves still moved
angrily, but their own ship was passing through quiet waters.

'I shall be glad when we reach King Brude's castle,' said
Jean, gravely. 'The Blue Men are too wet and strong. I don't
like it when they make the sea and the clouds come together.
And I was frightened when the wind went flooling by.'

'We shan't be long now,' answered Borrobil. 'Indeed, we
mustn't be long, or we shall be too late.'

'Too late for what?' cried Donald.

'Too late for the fight in which the White King must overthrow the Black King if summer is to reign again,' was the
reply.

CHAPTER 22

The End of a Voyage, and a Sad but a Great Farewell

THE Long Ship had been drawn beneath the angry waves and was now the Blue Men's spoil. So had they escaped a double danger. The Blue Men who might have dragged them to the deeps had let them pass; but more than that, the Blue Men had seized and claimed the foe's pursuing ship. And now, as they ran through quiet waters again, Donald and Jean once more found pleasure in every minute of their voyage.

For most of the time they were sailing close to the land, and for every rock, every castle, and every cave, Borrobil had a story ready to tell. This rock was the favourite basking-ground of the seals who once were men. That castle had been built to protect within its encircling wall a marvellous tree that in summer bore live geese instead of fruit, and as soon as the geese were full-grown they dropped to the ground, even as ripe fruit will drop; but there was this difference – that the geese had to be gathered at once before they could stretch their wings, otherwise they would fly away and be lost. That big black cave was the very cave in which a fisherman had long held captive a mermaid whose robe he had hidden away so that she was unable to return to the sea.

To all these, and many similar tales, the children listened with wondering eyes. Never was Borrobil at a loss. Once, when Donald had pointed to a bright light that flashed in and out on the side of a hill as it caught or lost the rays of the sun, Borrobil explained that the hill was really a giant who had but one eye and who had been chained to that very spot by a great magician hundreds of years ago, so that now the grass and the trees had grown all over him; and whilst to ordinary eyes he looked just

an ordinary hill, he could still be recognized as the captive
giant whenever the strong sunlight made him blink his one
eye, even as he was doing then! And once, when Jean had
cried out with delight at some graceful fishes that went gliding
by, Borrobil told her that they were the thirteen beautiful
daughters of King Iasgair who, when bathing in a pool on the
shore by the king's castle, had been changed into thirteen
fishes by a malignant spirit who hated them for their beauty;
and that they were condemned to live as fish in the sea until
they should be caught, all in the one net, by a fisherman who
was his mother's seventh child, when at once they would re-
sume their beautiful human forms again and the fisherman
would marry the youngest of them and would become the
master of all King Iasgair's ships.

So the time passed quickly by; the gentle waves ran quickly
past their ship; and almost too soon, if that were possible, they
caught a glimpse of King Brude's castle standing strong amid
the hills by the sea. And how proud the castle looked! No
longer did an air of gloom surround it, as in the days when the
dragon ruled the land. Now, from every turret and every tower,
bright standards flew bravely in the breeze. Four horsemen
stood on guard before the gate; and spearmen marched to and
fro upon the walls. Their ship was seen! The note of a horn
came sounding across the water. The gate of the castle was
thrown wide open. And almost as their prow grounded on the
beach, there stood King Brude with all his court and all his
people to welcome them.

Morac leapt into the breaking surf, and lifting Finella into
his arms carried her above the waves to her father the king.
Then was there tender greeting between them, and the salt
tears wet their eyes as they rejoiced to be together again.
Fondly King Brude embraced his daughter; fondly Finella
gazed upon her father. Each thought of the seven unhappy
years that had kept them apart; each thought of the many
happy years that now lay ahead. Their joy was complete.
Morac, his own eyes scarcely dry, returned to the ship. He
lifted Jean into his arms and carried her ashore. He made one

more journey for Donald; and this time, as he waded shore-
wards through the waves, Borrobil jumped merrily with him
by his side.

Now all of them stood around the king. There came a call
for silence. A hush fell upon the throng that had gathered there.
Then King Brude placed Finella's hand in Morac's, and cried

out in a firm voice, 'Witness all who are here present that today shall the noble Morac take the Princess Finella to be his bride.' Loud shouts rang through the air, and were echoed and re-echoed from the hills beyond. Again there came a call for silence. The king turned to Donald and Jean. From them he turned to the assembled crowd! Again he cried out in a firm voice – 'My people! No day, alas! is without its sorrow. The stranger children, so shortly our guests, must forthwith return to their own land. Their time is spent. Even now they tarry too long. Yet although they leave us today, in every tomorrow shall they be in our thoughts. For through them, too, has come this our present joy. To the stranger children we give our thanks. To the stranger children we pledge our thoughts. To the stranger children we bid a sad farewell.'

The king bent to kiss Jean's hand; he placed his own two hands between Donald's hands. Finella came forward and kissed both of them, and the tears were glistening within her eyes. Then came Morac. He lifted high above his head, for every man to see, first Jean, then Donald. And as they were lifted up, the shouts of the people broke forth again, and again the neighbouring hills made answer.

And what of Borrobil? For long he had been showing impatience in every move. Several times had he taken a few steps forward, only to take a few steps back again. Several times had he opened his mouth as if to say something, only to shut it again as if on second thoughts he had decided it would be better to keep silent. But now, when at last Morac put down the children after lifting them up for all to see, Borrobil could bear it no longer.

'We must go!' he cried. 'Or we shall indeed be too late.'

The king nodded. He gave a call; and the spearmen from the castle made a wide lane through the thronging crowd. Donald and Jean looked sadly round. Must they really go? Had they really to leave everyone like this, just when everything had come right? The dragon had been killed, the Black Sulig and the Giant Grugol had been slain, the men of the Long Ships had been defeated, and now Morac had brought

Finella back to her own kingdom to become his bride. Surely they could stay a little longer!

But again Borrobil called impatiently, 'Come!' and they knew that they would have to go. They gave one last lingering look at the king, at Finella, at Morac. All of them smiled a little wistfully at each other. Donald and Jean called out haltingly, regretfully, 'Good-bye!' The king and Morac raised their swords in salute. Greysteel flashed in the air, and, as it flashed, the blade seemed to ring out 'Good luck.' Finella blew a kiss with both her hands and turned quickly away.

Then Borrobil took their hands and hastened them down the lane between the spearmen standing on either side, between the people thronging deep beyond, and between the shouts that rang loud and long in one great farewell. They were setting forth on their last adventure.

CHAPTER 23

In which they Return to the Nine-Stone-Ring; the Black King of Winter Flees the Land; and Once More they Pass between the Beltane Fires

BORROBIL rushed them across the heather as fast as they could go. To their left stood the hill by the 'dragon's hollow'; and again Donald noticed the ridges made in the sides of the hill by the tightening grip of the dying monster. On; on! Now they were passing the lake in the midst of which stood the wooden island; but the island huts were deserted, for with the dragon's death the people could walk without fear through the length and breadth of all the land. And still Borrobil rushed them on. Jean thought of their rush through the forest when Sulig was beneath the ground, and now, as then, she felt 'all breathed-out' and 'blowing like a grand-puff'. She could go no farther.

'Stop!' she cried, 'I can't run any more.'

'And I'm almost breathless, too,' added Donald.

Borrobil stopped, and looked at them anxiously. Then he looked at the sky.

'There may yet be time,' he said; 'but we must make what haste we can. We dare not be late.'

So saying, he let go of the children's hands, and the three of them walked more slowly across the heath. In the distance they could see the outer edge of the wood. Soon they would reach the wood itself. Then were they to see the White King of Summer drive the Black King of Winter forth from the land. And what would happen then? And what if they were too late for the fight? Why daren't they be late?

Donald turned to Borrobil. 'Why daren't we be late?' he asked. 'And what happens when the White King defeats the Black King?'

Borrobil looked at him. 'We daren't be late', he said, 'because you must go back again from these times that are dead to the times in which you lived when first you passed between the Beltane Fires and when first Jean danced in the Nine-Stone-Ring. That is the answer. We must reach the Nine-Stone-Ring before the White King wins. If we can, I would like you to reach the Ring in time to see the fight. And then,' continued Borrobil sadly, 'then shall I leave you, and you will never see me again.'

'Oh, no!' cried Jean. 'You mustn't go. I don't want you to go.'

'There is no choice,' answered Borrobil. 'I am bound to leave you, and you are bound to return to the times in which you lived before we met.'

There was silence for a long while. By now they had reached the wood, and again Borrobil led the way unerringly through thicket and tangled growth. Donald and Jean felt sad at heart. Why was Borrobil bound to leave them? Why was it they had to leave King Brude and Finella and Morac? Yet Borrobil had said there was no choice.

And still Borrobil pushed on and on, always keeping ahead of them. He seemed almost anxious to be in front and alone, as though he were unwilling to talk. Could it be that Borrobil also was sad, as sad as they were?

As they moved through the wood Donald thought he began to recognize the way. Surely this was the way they had come from the Nine-Stone-Ring to Giric's earth-house? 'Giric the shoeless' who had once seemed so taciturn, but who had played such a marvellous trick on the nasty dwarf and who had fought so bravely to rescue Jean when the two men from the Long Ships had carried her off. But now Giric was far away

with the Men of Orc and waiting for broken bones to mend.
And Giric, too, they would never see again.

Then, suddenly, they saw that Borrobil had stopped. They
came up to him and stood beside him. They had reached the
Nine-Stone-Ring!

Slowly Borrobil walked to one of the big stones and stood
beside it on the outer side of the Ring. He beckoned the
children to join him, and as they came closer he took off his
hat and sweeping the ground with it made one of his deepest,
his gravest bows. But gone was the merry mischievous look.
Borrobil looked serious and sad; and the white owl's feather in
the tip of his hat seemed to droop limply, sadly, like a flag will
droop when the gay breezes have passed it by.

'We can sit here to watch,' he said, 'and we are just in time.
But now must I take my leave of you, for later I shall have no
chance to say, "Farewell." Soon I shall explain to you all that
you will see; but, before that, I would say how much I grieve
at our parting, and I would say, too, that never before have I
known stranger children as brave as you, or children I have
loved so well.' Again Borrobil bowed to them, seriously,
gravely; again the white owl's feather seemed to hang listless
and unhappy in the tip of his sweeping hat.

'But we shall miss you, too,' cried Jean. 'We shall miss you
lots and lots and lots.' And the tears were not far from her eyes.

'And we shall never meet anyone whom we shall like half
so much,' cried Donald. 'And if you'd only let us we would
stay with you ever so much longer.'

'That cannot be,' replied Borrobil. 'As I have said, there is
no choice. Yet our meeting has brought pleasure to all. Let us
remember the pleasure it brought when we have forgotten the
sadness of our parting. And now must you listen carefully to
all that I have to say. Here, within the Nine-Stone-Ring, the
White King of Summer will ride in from the east to challenge
the Black King of Winter. The White King will challenge him
to fight for his possession of the land. Then in from the west
will ride the Black King of Winter to answer the challenge, to
try to maintain his rule and to hold back Summer's advance.

Then will they fight. And then, as has happened so many countless times before, the White King of Summer will defeat the Black King of Winter. The Black King will turn and flee. He will flee to the other side of the earth taking with him his wintry hordes. There in turn will he rule until, on the other side of the earth, the White King of Summer shall again ride forth to meet him, shall again drive him out; when once more with his wintry hordes he will flee back here again. So it goes on, year after year. And so Winter rules the land first here, then on the other side of the earth, then here again.

'But as the Black King flees the Ring, so will the day end. The sun will sink with the Black King's fleeing. And yet will there be no twilight. You will see the day turn, on the instant, into the darkness of night. And as the Black King flees, as the day turns into night, so shall I have gone from you, and you will be back again in the times in which you lived before first you came to visit us. So will you pass from the times of Winter, the times that are dead, to the times of Summer, the times that live.'

Borrobil stopped. He looked questioningly at the children. Then the old mischievous smile played about the corners of his mouth, and he added, 'But it's been a great adventure, hasn't it?'

'Yes, Yes!' they cried. And as they smiled back at him Borrobil signalled to them to sit down and hide behind the stone.

The three of them settled down in their hiding-place. Borrobil and Jean on one side of the stone, Donald on the other. And scarcely had they settled down than they heard the sound of a horn. It was blown three times. And riding into the Ring from the east came two heralds on white horses.

'The heralds of Summer,' whispered Borrobil. 'Warm Wind and Gentle Rain. Always do they ride before the White King to announce his coming.'

The heralds rode round the Ring. Again they blew their horns. And in from the east rode the White King of Summer. He, too, rode a white steed; his armour was of gold, his shield was a bright blue, and his helmet seemed to be crowned with a wreath of green leaves. And as he rode into the Ring so his heralds turned and rode out to the east again, there taking up their stand outside the Ring by the very stones through which the King had come.

'The White King rides a white horse,' whispered Borrobil. 'His armour is of gold, for gold is the summer corn; his shield is bright blue, for bright blue is the summer sky; and his crest is a sprig of the green oak leaves.'

The White King rode proudly round the Ring. He turned,

and rode to its very centre. There he reined in his steed, and lifting his sword on high called out in a loud voice –

'*Hear, O Black King of Winter, defender in this combat. Appear forthwith to defend thyself and thy rule against the White King of Summer who hath come to meet thee.*'

There was no answer. Again the White King rode proudly round the Ring. Again he rode to its very centre. Again he called forth his challenge, and this time he ended with the words –

'*The day passeth; therefore come without delay.*'

Still there was no answer. Once more the White King rode proudly round the Ring. Once more he rode to its very centre.

Once more he called forth his challenge, and this time he ended with the words –

'*Appear in haste; for the day is wellnigh spent. Appear if thou wouldst maintain thyself within this land. Appear to defend thy rule before the sun goeth down.*'

And with that the White King turned his horse and rode to the eastern side of the Ring.

Then, even as the White King reached the side of the Ring and turned again, there to take up his stand facing the centre of the Ring, so, from the west, came the sound of a horn. It was blown three times. And riding into the Ring from the western side came two heralds on black horses.

'The heralds of Winter,' whispered Borrobil. 'Bitter Frost and Raging Storm. Always do they ride before the Black King to announce his coming.'

Again the heralds of Winter blew their horns, and in from the west rode the Black King. He, too, rode a black steed; his armour was red rust; his shield was dull and dark; and his helmet was crowned with white. And as he rode into the Ring so his heralds turned and rode out to the west again, there taking up their stand outside the Ring by the very stones through which the king had come.

'The Black King rides a black horse,' whispered Borrobil. 'His armour is of the red rust that eats and gnaws; his shield is dull and dark as the days of his rule; and his crest is the white frost that he lays over all the land.'

Straight to the centre of the Ring rode the Black King. There he reined in his horse, and lifting his sword on high called out in a loud voice:

> '*Who would drive me from the land?*
> *Here let him stand.*
> *Here let him strike with all his might,*
> *Ere day be night.*'

And the Black King turned his horse and rode to the western side of the Ring, there to take up his stand.

And now the White King once more rode to the centre of

the Ring. He in turn held high his sword and called out in a
firm voice:

> *'Here I stand;*
> *'Tis I shall drive Black Winter from the land.*
> *'Tis I shall drive him forth in headlong flight.*
> *Ere day be night.'*

The White King brandished his sword, and holding his horse
firm on the rein stayed in the very centre of the Ring. Then
from the western side the Black King spurred his horse and
rode to meet him. In the centre of the Ring they met. In the
centre of the Ring their swords crossed.

The Black King pressed in, hard and furious. His onslaught
was like the winter's gale that would bear all down before it.
Thick and fast fell his blows, and as they fell they seemed to
strike sunbeams and sunlight from the White King's armour.
But despite the fury of the onslaught, still the White King
stood fast. Then, once, the Black King paused as though his
fury had outspent itself. And as he paused, so the White King
bore down upon him. His own sword fell hard and true upon
the Black King's helm. Snow and ice were scattered around.
Still the White King struck hard and oft. The Black King sank
low within his saddle. He swayed. He seemed about to fall.
But, making one last effort, he regained his seat, and turning
his steed, galloped madly in headlong flight towards the
western side of the Ring, and so out towards the lowering
sun.

Through the dark network of trees the sun seemed to be
balancing like a fiery ball upon the edge of the distant land.
For one brief moment that fiery ball blazed round and full;
with the next moment, as the Black King galloped madly from
the Ring, the fiery ball had gone. And even as Borrobil had
warned the children, so, with the sinking of the sun, they
passed at once from the bright light of day to the blackness of
night. The change was as quick and sudden as that other
change, so long ago, when Jean had danced in this selfsame
ring, when the darkness of night had changed on the instant

into the grey light of dawn, and Borrobil had called out 'Good morning.'

Donald and Jean sat up, as if roused from sleep. Half-frightened, they called out 'Borrobil! Borrobil!' But there was no answer. Only a night-bird called from the trees above; only the rustling leaves responded. 'Borrobil!' they called. But this time, somehow, they felt less certain of themselves, as though they knew it was foolish to call, foolish to expect an answer. What did it all mean? When they had first met Borrobil the night had turned to day. Now that Borrobil had gone – gone as mysteriously as he had come – the day had turned to night. What could it mean?

As they sat there, wondering, Donald heard a faint call in the distance. He looked at Jean and saw that she, too, had heard something. Both of them listened. It came again; and this time it was nearer. There could be no mistake. Someone, something, had called out somewhere in the depths of the wood. Yet in some way the call sounded strangely familiar; it sounded like a call they had heard before. And now the night seemed to be less dark. Why was that? The moon, of course! There it was, shining in the sky above and almost at the full. But why had they not noticed it before? And what was that strange and different light that danced on the standing stones of the Ring? They turned round, and there, burning bright before mound and ring were two fires of blazing pine-logs.

Had they dreamt it all? Had they just fallen asleep by one of the stones in the Nine-Stone-Ring? Donald stood up. Unconsciously he put his hands into the pockets of his coat. Then, quickly, he withdrew them again. There was a startled look on his face. His biscuits! They were not there! 'Jean!' he cried excitedly. 'Jean! Have you still got your lucky-stone?'

Jean was already on her feet and standing beside him. She felt feverishly, frantically, first in this pocket, then in that. But nowhere could she find her lucky-stone. Then she remembered. 'Of course I haven't,' she said. 'I gave it to Honest Haff to carry Giric like a sack of meal on his back.'

She paused. But had she?

They looked at one another. Certainly Donald no longer had his three biscuits. Certainly Jean no longer had her lucky-stone. How then could they have dreamt it all?

They walked slowly from the Ring and down the steps of the mound. Once more they walked between the fires of blazing pine-logs. As they passed through the fires, again there came a call. This time it was quite close. Another call. A shout. They saw a group of men standing beneath the trees. The men seemed to be pointing to them. Now the men were coming slowly towards them.

Donald and Jean stopped. For the first time they felt afraid. They turned as if to run back. Then Donald gave a cry. He took Jean's hand in his. In the light of the fires he had recognized the men. They were the men from their own village, the village in which they were staying. Holding hands they stood still before the blazing fires.

Slowly the men approached. They walked cautiously, carefully, almost as though they were uncertain of something that lay ahead. So they drew nearer until, suddenly, one of them called out, and in a voice of sharp surprise:

'Why! It's Donald and Jean!'

One of the men broke away from the others and ran up to them. It was Hamish, the shepherd.

'Where have you come from?' he cried.

'From the Nine-Stone-Ring,' answered Donald.

'The Nine-Stone-Ring!' Now the men had crowded round them, and everyone seemed to be saying the words at once. 'The Nine-Stone-Ring! And on Beltane Eve!'

'Yes,' replied the children, looking at the men, wonderingly.

The men from the village turned to one another. Heads were shaken and there were low murmurs. Then Jean spoke:

'Ah! but Borrobil was looking after us,' she said.

'Borrobil?' repeated the men, 'Borrobil?'

And now an old man held up his hand. There was silence as all turned to him, waiting for his words.

'Borrobil!' he said. 'I remember that name. Once my great-grandsire spoke it when I was but a little boy. And then he said something about magic and the times of long ago. And that, too, had something to do with passing between the Beltane Fires. I was only a boy then, yet I well remember the name. But who Borrobil was I've forgotten now, and I doubt if I ever rightly knew.'

The old man paused. His voice dropped to a mumble. Now he seemed to be talking to himself.

But Donald and Jean looked at one another with bright and sparkling eyes:

Borrobil! They knew! And they would never forget!

A NOTE FOR THE CURIOUS
OR AN ANSWER TO A QUESTION

BELTANE was the great Celtic festival held at the beginning of May. Then the people put out all their fires and gathered together to make new fire for the coming year. This they did by the violent friction of two pieces of wood – usually two very large pieces of wood so that many men had to take part in the task. The fire made in this way was known as 'need fire'; from the 'need fire' two Beltane Fires were lit; and from the Beltane Fires all the hearth-fires were in turn rekindled.

The Beltane Fires were lit on some one particular hill in each district, and in the lighting of them teams of nine men, twenty-seven men, or even as many as eighty-one men were used to make the 'need fire'. But the number of men in the fire-team was always in a 'progression' of three.

Many special virtues were attributed to the two Beltane Fires. To pass between them was at one time an ordeal; at another time it was held to give protection during the coming year against disease or ill-luck.

Probably Beltane can be traced back to the worship of fire or to sun-worship. But the time of the festival and many of the rites which were observed also indicate a thanksgiving for the return of summer. Summer and winter meant far more to the people of the past than they mean to us. Then, summer meant life and food; winter might well mean the opposite. And certain similar ceremonies at the beginning of November, when summer passed and winter came, were possibly intended to secure the return of summer in the following year.

Beltane Eve was the night preceding Beltane. Then supernatural events were supposed to take place. The Fairies, for example, rode to their great May-day gathering; and dew collected on Beltane Eve possessed certain magical properties.

Apparently the Beltane Fires were lit sometimes on Beltane Eve and sometimes on Beltane. In the story, they had been lit on Beltane Eve; and Donald and Jean passed between them just as Beltane Eve was giving way to Beltane. Thus the time, the place, and what the children did, all combined to form, in the words of Borrobil, 'the most magic-making thing I know'.

If you have enjoyed this book and would like to know about others which we publish, why not join the Puffin Club? You will receive the club magazine, *Puffin Post*, four times a year and a smart badge and membership book. You will also be able to enter all the competitions. For details of cost and an application form, send a stamped addressed envelope to:

The Puffin Club, Dept. A
Penguin Books Limited
Bath Road
Harmondsworth
Middlesex